Haunted Inns of the Southeast

The photograph used on the cover and the facing page is of Oak Alley Plantation, Vacherie, Louisiana.
COURTESY OF OAK ALLEY PLANTATION

Haunted Inns

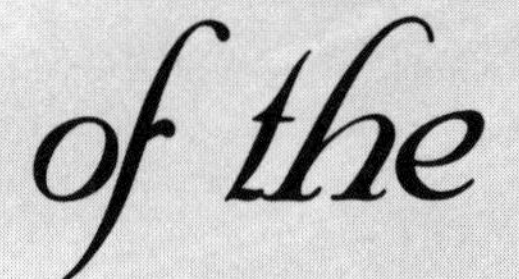

of the Southeast

SHEILA TURNAGE

JOHN F. BLAIR, PUBLISHER WINSTON-SALEM, NORTH CAROLINA

Published by John F. Blair, Publisher

*The paper in this book meets the guidelines
for permanence and durability of the
Committee on Production Guidelines for
Book Longevity of the Council on Library Resources.*

Library of Congress Cataloging-in-Publication Data

Turnage, Sheila.
Haunted inns of the Southeast / Sheila Turnage.
p. cm.
Includes index.
ISBN 0-89587-234-X (alk. paper)
1. Haunted hotels—Southern States. 2. Ghosts—Southern States.
3. Apparitions—Southern States. I. Title.

BF1474.5.T87 2001
133.1'0975—dc21
2001018490

Design by Debra Long Hampton

For those who care enough to linger. . .

Contents

Acknowledgments

Many people contributed to the creation of this book, and I am grateful to each of them.

As always, I owe my first thanks to my first reader and fellow traveler, Rodney L. Beasley, for his input, patience, and attention to detail.

Thanks also to my agent, Deidre Knight of the Knight Agency, who helped create a framework for the project, and offered sound advice throughout.

Many people at John F. Blair, Publisher, graciously contributed their talents and efforts to this project, and I thank them all. President Carolyn Sakowski provided excellent overall perspective for the project and also helped to gather the book's photos. Editor Steve Kirk judiciously pruned my prose and contributed to the articles' formatting. Designer Debbie Hampton gave the pages and cover their balance and style.

I gratefully acknowledge *Our State* magazine, which published my account of Asheville's Pink Lady in October 1998. A very similar version of that story appears here. I also thank *Our State* editor Mary Ellis for her enthusiasm for the original piece. My encounter with the Pink Lady, the ghost-in-residence at the Grove Park Inn, helped me imagine the book you now hold in your hands.

I offer my thanks to ghost researchers Joshua Warren and Janis Raley for talking to me about their work.

Finally, and perhaps most importantly, I thank the innkeepers and their staffs who took time to talk with me about their ghosts and ghost stories—especially the innkeepers who are allowing their stories to appear in print here for the very first time. Without their willingness to share their experiences and stories, this book could never have been written.

Introduction
Things to Know Before You Go

In this book, you'll find scores of great inns with good ghost stories. Some innkeepers host famous ghosts and tell well-known ghost stories. In other cases, innkeepers or their staffs tell their ghost stories in print here for the very first time.

I've listed inns reporting all levels of activity for readers interested in different experiences. You'll find everything from spirits who occasionally tread a distant staircase to energies who ring down for room service or dismantle guest-room doorknobs.

Each listing provides the basic ghost story and pinpoints the most active area of the inn, if possible. You may want to stay in the most haunted part of the building, or you may not. Ask yourself where your curiosity and comfort level truly overlap. *If your goal is to spend the night with a ghost, consider whom you want to wake up with.*

Ghost Speak

We have many words for ghostly phenomena. Some sound scary, some sound friendly, some sound scientific. I employ three terms in this book: *ghost, spirit,* and *energy*, and I use them interchangeably to describe the same phenomena.

Documenting Activity

No one really knows what ghosts are, but most people know when they have them. They hear footsteps, see doors open and close. Their lights and water turn on and off unexpectedly. The temperature may drop abruptly. Physical items may meander around the house. People may report an uneasiness in parts of the house; cats may look permanently frizzed. According to folks who live and work with them, ghosts pace, play, sing, joke, talk with people or each other, and even touch the people around them.

What are they?

Janis Raley, a professional historian and a founder of the Ghost Preservation League in Dallas, has been investigating ghosts for twenty-five years, and she still can't quite define them. "We don't try to do anything but document activity," she says. "I am not in the business of explaining it, because I don't really think you can. I don't say what it is, beyond energy."

Raley and other investigators use magnetometers to measure that energy; you'll find several references to magnetometer readings in this book. This is the electromagnetic energy that can make the hair on your arms or the back of your neck stand up when you're in an active area. It may also be the same energy that makes lights and spigots turn themselves on and off, or makes watches and clocks stop working, or shows up in photographs.

My own sense, having spoken with scores of people who live and work around ghosts, is that in addition to their physical properties, many spirits have an emotional connection to the people, places, and events around them.

You will no doubt draw your own conclusions.

Research

Although no inn can guarantee you'll witness any activity, a little research will improve your chances, according to Raley. "If you want to visit haunted places, try to go near an anniversary of things that happened there," she says. The anniversary may be of an emotional event particular to the inn (a death, for instance) or of an emotional event that imprinted the area in general (like a battle).

An example? "In Vicksburg, I go during the spring because it's way more active," Raley says, noting that the Battle of Vicksburg was fought in the springtime. Even if a Vicksburg inn doesn't have a specific Civil War history, the overall activity in the area may increase the activity in the inn, she explains.

If you can't pinpoint an anniversary, Raley suggests visiting during a full moon, when "things are much more intense."

What to Bring

Bring a camera with a flash.

"I've gotten shots with all kinds of cameras. You just need a really good flash, even in the daytime," Raley says, explaining that the flash bounces off the energy. "I've got [photos] without a flash, but that increases your chances."

Although she's collected good shots with a variety of cameras, Raley prefers digital cameras. She gets her best results with a Sony Mavica. "That's what I use 90 percent of the time," she says.

"Another thing, and it's fairly inexpensive, is a voice-activated tape recorder. If you're spending the night, just put it on and see what you get. But make sure all the lights are on when you listen to it," she laughs.

Bring extra batteries for the camera and recorder. Energies in very active areas can suck batteries dry, Raley says.

What to Do: Breathe

If you're in a haunted inn and unusual things start happening, please remember to breathe. "That's what I train people to do—breathe," Raley says. "Don't hold your breath."

When you see something outside your everyday experience, it's normal to hold your breath. But in this case, it's not particularly helpful. "You get a physiological response," she says. "If you can breathe through it, you can experience [the phenomenon] and not panic."

Relax and pay attention to your senses—all of them.

Haunted places harbor unusual energy, and different people register this energy in different ways. Some people see ghosts, some hear them, and some smell them. Some register the energy physically, while others sense a presence emotionally.

I don't know why some people see ghosts and others don't. It may just be the way we are tuned. Perhaps, it's no more mysterious than the fact that some people see a full spectrum of color, while others are colorblind.

Whatever your experience, Raley recommends recording soon after it happens, while the details remain fresh in your mind.

Worldly Information

This book is organized by state, starting in Louisiana and heading west to Florida, then meandering north to Virginia and down to Tennessee. Each chapter opens with a feature on a particularly interesting ghostly stopover. In these features, the contact information falls at the end of the story.

Following the feature, I've entered the state's other haunted inns alphabetically under their town or city name. When a town has more than one haunted inn, the inns are also arranged alphabetically within the heading.

Some inns have so many stories that they deserve their own book. The innkeeper or staff can often give you additional information if you ask.

When you're collecting information, please be considerate of the inn as a business. While some places listed in this book actively promote their ghost stories, others do not. Please remember that what intrigues you may unsettle other guests.

The rates for each inn reflect the cost of a double for one night. The key is:

$ = $100 or less
$$ = $100–$200
$$$ = $200–$300
$$$$ = over $300

Some rates are seasonal, so you may find variations. Always ask for details.

Finally, although this is the most complete guide of its kind on the market, it's inevitable that I've left out a haunted inn here or there. In a handful of cases, innkeepers were not willing to talk with me on the record about their ghost stories. I omitted those places out of respect for the innkeepers and for my readers. And despite my best efforts, I may have accidentally overlooked some other worthy listings.

If you know of other haunted inns, hotels, or bed-and-breakfasts, please let me know by writing me in care of the publisher. Thanks!

Publisher's contact information:

John F. Blair, Publisher
1406 Plaza Drive
Winston-Salem, North Carolina 27103
1-800-222-9796
blairpub@blairpub.com
FAX: 1-336-768-9194

Haunted Inns of the Southeast

LOUISIANA

Louisiana, the South's most culturally diverse state, abounds in ghost stories. You'll find haunted inns, hotels, and bed-and-breakfasts from one side of the state to the other, and an embarrassment of riches, almost, in New Orleans, the most openly haunted city in the United States.

Interestingly enough, though, Louisiana's best-known haunted inn isn't in New Orleans. Myrtles Plantation resides in St. Francisville, a tiny historic town on the Great River Road between New Orleans and Natchez, Mississippi. St. Francisville, population eighteen hundred, has over 140 buildings listed on the National Register and claims one of the largest concentrations of antebellum homes in the nation. In turn, Myrtles Plantation claims one of the state's highest concentrations of ghosts.

Myrtles Plantation

7747 U.S. 61 North
St. Francisville, LA 70775
800-809-0565 or 225-635-6277
$$

Murder at the Myrtles

Hester Eby's workaday life isn't quite like yours and mine. Since around 1985, Eby's been a tour guide at Myrtles Plantation, one of the most haunted inns in the United States. "Sometimes you just get a peaceful feeling. It's just a normal feeling and a normal day," she says, reflecting on her workplace. "But sometimes you know things are not quite right."

In fact, goings-on at The Myrtles have been "not quite right" for a good while now. This elegant old home has witnessed ten murders over the past two hundred years, and most of the victims' spirits still whisper about the house.

Some folks meet them before they even reach the door. According to Eby, guests sometimes arrive to report that "a white man in overalls and a straw hat has met them at the front gate." This fellow can be a bit testy. Guests complain that "he's been quiet rude and will not let them in," she says.

Other visitors pass the gate easily enough but see two girls playing on the lawn, especially on rainy days. "They're wearing long, white dresses and have long, blond hair," Eby says. Despite the downpour, they're never wet. There's a reason: they died here some 150 years ago.

The Myrtles' disquiet started long before these little girls met their violent fate.

General David Bradford chose this site for his home in the late 1700s, sweeping generations of Native American history aside to

make way for his mansion. "This used to be the Tunica burial grounds," Eby says, referring to a Native American people who once lived along the Mississippi. "It's believed when General Bradford, the first owner, bought this land, he cleared it, piled the [Tunicas' dead] to the side, and burned the remains. That's one reason people believe the ground was cursed."

Bradford, who moved into this plantation house in 1796, seems to have escaped the curse. But nightmarish luck moved into the plantation house with the next occupants.

Judge Clarke Woodruffe bought the house around 1820 and brought his young bride to The Myrtles. "Sarah Matilda . . . was very young, about fourteen," Eby says. "Shortly after they were married, he took a mistress, who was one of his house servants."

That mistress, a slave named Chloe, worked in the main house. Information meant power to Chloe. One night, she crouched by the judge's door, listening to a conversation between husband and wife, who by then had two daughters. The judge surprised her at

Below, note the ghost of Chloe standing between the two buildings. In the close-up shot at right, notice that the image of Chloe is transparent.
COURTESY OF THE MYRTLES PLANTATION

the door. "She had been warned about eavesdropping," Eby says in a hushed voice. As punishment, Woodruffe had Chloe's left ear sliced from her head.

After that, Chloe wore a green turban to hide her disfigurement. She bided her time, and she planned. When the judge went to New Orleans, Chloe made her move. She baked his young daughter a birthday cake and added the juice of an oleander leaf to its batter. Oleander's effects mimic arsenic's, Eby says.

Did she plan to kill the children? According to plantation lore, the answer is no. "I think she really thought she could make them ill and then save them," says Eby. Her heroism would prove her value to the family and secure her place in the household.

It didn't work out that way. The birthday girl blew out her scant handful of candles and shared her cake with her mother and sister. If Chloe could have prevented their agonizing deaths, she didn't.

"After she confessed to what she had done, she was killed by an angry mob," Eby says. They hanged her and fed her body to the Mississippi.

Chloe didn't take death lying down.

"A lot of people say they see Chloe," Eby says. "From the shoulders down, [the apparition] is misty but the figure of a woman. From the shoulders up, she's a black woman with a large earring in her right ear, and her left ear missing." She still hides her disfigurement with a green turban.

Visitors often see the two girls, ages five and seven, playing in the rain. "People notice they aren't wet," Eby says. Some people believe the girls enter this world through a mirror bearing their handprints.

Their mother's spirit resides here, too. "Mostly, Sarah Matilda is known by different smells—like honeysuckle or roses. It may have been some type of perfume she wore," Eby says. "The smell is there, and then the sound of crying is usually there."

Bad luck followed the next family who owned The Myrtles, too. The Ruffin Grey Sterlings "accumulated over five thousand acres and over a hundred slaves," Eby says. Along with it, they reaped an eternity of grief.

Their son died in the dining room, stabbed to death over a

gambling debt. He fell by the door. Even though the floor is kept bare, visitors often trip over the spot, Eby says. Electrical appliances meet resistance there, too, as if repelled by magnets. "The buffer will push away," she says. "If you're sweeping, it's okay, but if you're using the vacuum, it pushes away."

The Sterlings' bad luck didn't die with their son. When eight-year-old Kate came down with yellow fever, the family put her to bed and, in desperation, sent to a nearby plantation for an enslaved woman reputed to be a voodoo priestess, hoping she could save the beloved child. Despite the woman's efforts, Kate died. And the priestess? "They killed her," Eby says.

Today, some visitors staying in Kate's room, now called the William Winters Room, wake up feeling feverish. Naturally, they push the covers away. When they awaken again, they find themselves tucked neatly into bed, their covers smoothed by unseen hands. "Some will leave in the middle of the night," Eby chuckles. Others report hearing a child's voice in the room, or a woman saying the Lord's Prayer.

The ghost on their staircase has his own bad-luck tale. Attorney William Winters, who married the Sterlings' daughter, was here one night when someone rode into the yard, calling his name. "He went out on the porchway, and whoever called for him shot him in the chest with a shotgun," Eby says. Winters struggled toward his wife, who was upstairs. "He tried to reach her. He only made it to the seventeenth step." He died in his wife's arms. "A lot of guests have told us that they can hear a lady's voice cry there, that they can hear footsteps go up those stairs, but not down. Some say they've heard the [front] door slam."

Other less active spirits at The Myrtles include a tutor shot by carpetbaggers during the Civil War, and the spirit of a Confederate soldier.

As for the surly overseer who greets guests at the gate, he occupied the caretaker's cottage until 1927, when someone stabbed him. "No one reported seeing him until the 1960s," Eby says, noting that the ghost began walking after workers tore his cottage down. A new cottage went up in its place. "It's an overnight guest room now, and some people say they see the shape of a man looking out the windows in their photographs." Some people react strongly to the cottage and ask for other accommodations.

The Myrtles is furnished with antiques. Rates include a continental breakfast, a complimentary tour of the plantation house, and a discount on Friday and Saturday "Mystery Tours."

You have a good chance of bumping into a spirit no matter which of the eleven guest rooms you choose. Several guests have reported photographing a woman on the staircase and the overseer in the cottage, so bring a camera. In addition to the phenomena already mentioned, employees report empty rocking chairs rocking, doors opening and closing, and conversations in empty rooms.

As for Eby, she's accepted that her work life includes catching glimpses of people who lived hundreds of years ago and hearing spirits speak to her. "I'm very comfortable with knowing that, without a doubt, there's something here," she says.

CHENEYVILLE

Loyd Hall Plantation

292 LOYD BRIDGE ROAD
CHENEYVILLE, LA 71325
800-240-8135 OR 318-776-5641
www.louisianatravel.com/loyd_hall
$-$$

"I've worked here in this house for twenty-eight years," says Beulah Davis, a tour guide at Loyd Hall. "I've had a lot of experiences with the ghosts here."

Davis didn't believe in ghosts when she first came to Loyd Hall. "When I can sense something moving, and I'm the only person in the house—that's what made me change my mind," she says. "There's not anything evil," she adds quickly. "Just enough to let you know they're here."

For instance, the several spirits residing in this antebellum mansion often adjust the table before meals. "When we set tables, there's always something missing—silverware, a napkin, or glass . . . We'll find it in another room. They're kind of on the mischievous side," Davis says.

The spirit of owner William Loyd still makes himself at home here, even though Federal soldiers hanged him during the Civil War. "He's the major one. We hear footsteps," she says.

"Sometimes we get a glimpse of a black woman dressed in white. Sally Boston was a slave nanny that lived in the house with the family at that time. The nannies always wore a white dress." According to local lore, Boston was poisoned, which may explain why she's often accompanied by the smell of food. "We get a whiff of food cooking," Davis says. "You'll smell food when nothing's on the stove."

The spirit of William Loyd's niece, Inez, also dwells here. In fact, that's probably Inez restlessly trailing her finger along the keys

William Loyd, his niece Inez, a slave named Sally Boston, and a musician named Harry all reside at Loyd Hall Plantation.
COURTESY OF LOYD HALL PLANTATION

of the piano in the main hall. "A lot of times, we hear somebody rub their fingers across the keys, but there's nobody out there," Davis says. "She was engaged to be married. Her fiancé deserted her. She either jumped or was pushed out the third-floor window."

Finally, there's Harry, a musician who deserted from the Union army to hide in the attic of the then-abandoned Loyd Hall. When the family returned and discovered him—well, let's just say there's blood on the floor and a shallow grave beneath the house. "At midnight, Harry returns and plays his violin," Davis says. "He comes down to the second floor."

Harry's still a tad high-strung. Once, the staff took a group upstairs to Harry's hiding place. They couldn't get in. "There was a chest of drawers jammed against the door from the inside," Davis says.

Not surprisingly, guests report unusual experiences here, from seeing apparitions, to feeling walls vibrate, to hearing screams in the night. Bowls slide across the dining-room table; doors open and shut; lights flip on and off. "You'll see the rocking chair rocking. You get a glimpse of the clothes, the long dresses, the long coats . . ."

One visitor had her dress altered while she wore it. "The whole hem started to unravel. She could just see the thread coming out of her dress," Davis chuckles. "A lot of this happens in daytime. Midday, morning, afternoon, anytime . . .

"I always tell everybody, people can tell you about these things, but you have to personally experience this for yourself and make up your own mind. Some people are born to be able to experience this, and some people are not." In case you're not, watch the cats. Their hair stands up when the spirits troop by.

This historic inn has six guest rooms and pleasant, old-timey gardens. It's furnished with antiques throughout. You have the best chance of meeting a ghost if you book room 2, 3, or 4—all original rooms of the 1820 plantation house.

The spirit Amelie, who haunts T'Frere's House and Garconniere is often seen wearing a long, rose-colored dress.
COURTESY OF T'FRERE'S HOUSE AND GARCONNIERE

T'Frere's House and Garconniere

1905 VEROT SCHOOL ROAD
LAFAYETTE, LA 70508
800-984-9347
$$

Maugie and Pat Pastor didn't realize this 1880 Acadian Colonial home was haunted when they bought it in 1994. But they soon met the spirit of Amelie, a young schoolteacher who lived here a century ago. "She's more mischievous than mean," Maugie says. "I call her *canaille*. That's French. It means conniving."

Amelie, a petite woman often seen wearing a long, rose-colored dress, lost her husband early in life. One day, she went to the well to wash her face. "Whether she was pushed down the well or jumped to her death, no one knows," Maugie says. When the Catholic Church ruled the death a suicide, Amelie's body was buried outside the church cemetery.

Maugie believes Amelie roams the house, waiting to be released from life on earth. "Some of the guests have encountered her in

You might see Amelie roaming this hallway, waiting to be released from life on earth.
COURTESY OF T'FRERE'S HOUSE AND GARCONNIERE

different ways," she says. Amelie walks the garden paths, rattles pots in the pantry, turns lights off and on, opens and closes doors, and—if the Pastors discuss her—sometimes sets off the burglar alarm. "That's why I don't like to talk about her too much," Maugie says.

Like many spirits, Amelie doesn't like to see her home changed. "Anytime we change anything, she will manifest herself and get upset," Maugie says.

Amelie can be helpful, too. Earlier owners claimed she helped their son with his homework, nursed family members through the flu, and even awakened the family when the house caught fire, ensuring their safety. She enjoys nice things and has been known to lay out women's lingerie. On the other hand, she dislikes hymns and spatters wax on the piano if anyone plays them—possibly a comment on the Church's view of her death.

Amelie's home is now a friendly bed-and-breakfast reflecting the Pastors' Cajun culture. It's noted for its Cajun breakfasts, "T'juleps," and gardens.

New Orleans

New Orleans easily ranks as the most haunted city in the Southeast. The reasons? Fever and fire.

The French founded New Orleans in the early 1700s, populating their New World city in part from their Old World prisons. Spanish, African, and island cultures later added their bloodlines and beliefs to the city's rich culture.

Several times in the eighteenth and nineteenth centuries, fires raced through New Orleans, gobbling up buildings and consuming lives. Deadlier still were the fevers that rose from the Louisiana bayous in summer.

As you might expect, the South's most haunted city supports a variety of ghost tours. Check with your bed-and-breakfast for recommendations.

Andrew Jackson Hotel

919 Royal Street, New Orleans, LA 70116
800-654-0224 or 504-561-5881
www.historicinnsneworleans.com
$-$$

Local ghost tours often spotlight this hotel, but night manager Thomas Bowles didn't find out about the nightlife here until after he reported for duty in 1998. "When I first started here, I had no idea what was going on," he says.

He found out a few days later. "The hotel was completely empty, and I heard a loud crashing and banging, like someone was going nuts," he recalls. "I ran upstairs and found . . . nothing. I ran up those stairs like a bolt. There was not a soul up there."

The reason? The Andrew Jackson Hotel hosts an energetic troupe of child ghosts.

"From what I've seen, it goes way back to when [the building] used to be an orphanage," Bowles says. Tragically, a fire claimed

The Andrew Jackson Hotel hosts an energetic troupe of child ghosts.
COURTESY OF THE ANDREW JACKSON HOTEL

the lives of at least eighteen African American orphans who lived here.

They're still at home in the building. The children, who often zip through the lobby, become increasingly boisterous when the hotel has only a few rooms occupied—an infrequent event here, even in the off-season. On these nights, the children turn the courtyard into their playground. "I get complaints from guests," Bowles says. "Usually, it's in the wee hours of the morning, between two and three, sometimes as late as four. It's always the back rooms." One guest even called the desk to complain about a child bouncing a ball against his door.

"Occasionally, I'll get a call from 211 or 111, which face the courtyard, asking me to keep the children quiet. And of course, there are no children." He sighs. "Every time that happens, my blood runs cold. To have someone who has no knowledge call you, angry, and ask you to keep the children quiet . . . It's a little unnerving."

Bowles never checks the courtyard at those times. "I don't go in the courtyard when I get complaints like that. I *don't* go into the courtyard," he says emphatically. "As long as they leave me alone, they can have their run of the courtyard."

As for the customers, Bowles feels he can't gracefully introduce the concept of ghosts at three in the morning. "You have to tell them *something*, and you can't always tell them the truth. What I can tell them is that the Quarter is unusual, and the acoustics are strange, and what they're hearing may be miles away. Every time it happens, my blood runs cold because these are people that have no idea as to the history of the hotel. . . . You know it's not someone just trying to make a joke."

Although courtyard ball games are rare, the children's excursions in the hotel are not. "I'm always seeing what I call fleeting shadows," Bowles says. "You look up and see something disappear into the walls, or into the crack of the wall. That's so commonplace it doesn't even unnerve me anymore. That's a nightly occurrence."

A small delegation of child spirits recently approached Bowles. "That was one of the . . . most unnerving things that happened to me." He was at his desk when he realized he was being watched. "When I looked up, I saw just the tops of their heads—like children, like they're trying to peep over the desk. It didn't really scare me. It just startled the you-know-what out of me. And then, poof! They were gone. It's like they melt into the wall or disappear into the wall. I couldn't say where they go, they go so fast. It wasn't really frightening. It was just unnerving and startling. The most recent things that happened are things have turned up missing, and then moved. I will put a pen down, and when I [try to] pick it up, it's missing."

This twenty-two-room hotel offers complimentary continental breakfasts and easy access to the French Quarter. "All the major attractions within the Quarter are walkable," Bowles says. The hotel has no parking, but clerks will gladly direct guests to convenient pay lots.

You have the best chance of hearing the child spirits playing in the courtyard in the summer, during the off-season. Ask for a room on the courtyard. You might also try Room 208.

"Room 208 is always a problem," Bowles says, adding that a boy committed suicide in the room, and guests sometimes sense a presence there. "Desk clerks have described times when guests have checked into 208 and checked right out. We have had maids in housekeeping that would not go into that room," Bowles says. It's also not unusual for someone to adjust the lights when the room is unoccupied, switching control from a switch by the door to a pull chain on the fixture.

Some people claim Andrew Jackson's ghost visits the hotel that bears his name, but Bowles scoffs at the notion. "I am sure that man has better things to do than run around an old hotel at night," he says.

The Bourbon Orleans Hotel

THE BOURBON ORLEANS HOTEL
717 ORLEANS STREET
NEW ORLEANS, LA 20116
504-523-2222; www.bourbonorleans.com
$-$$$

In the 1800s, the elegant Bourbon Orleans Hotel hosted the city's Quadroon Balls, which introduced beautiful young African American–Creole women to society and often waltzed them into the arms of young white aristocrats. "Young men, before marrying age, would take on a mistress to learn the ways of love and romance," explains Rob Phillips, reservation manager for the hotel. Those relationships rarely led to marriage, as two of the ill-fated lovers who haunt this historic hotel could tell you.

"A man, during the time of the Civil War, met a mistress here at the Bourbon Orleans Hotel," Phillips says. "He went off to fight the Civil War, and he had promised her that if and when he returned, he would meet her here, and they would be married."

He never returned. "He died in battle, and she was so distraught that she actually committed suicide. It's said that in the ballroom, sometimes you can see [them] searching for each other. She is often spotted inside the ballroom looking out the window." Her lover, in his Confederate uniform, "is in the reception area of the ballroom. They're seen maybe a couple times a year," Phillips says.

In the 1800s, the Bourbon Orleans Hotel hosted the city's Quadroon Balls.
COURTESY OF THE BOURBON ORLEANS HOTEL

Some people will see the hotel's chandeliers swinging.
COURTESY OF THE BOURBON ORLEANS HOTEL

"Some people will see our chandeliers swinging," he adds.

A third spirit from that era returns here as well, possibly hoping to redress a heartbreak of a different kind. "They had a couple parlor rooms on the other side of the reception area, where people would have poker games," Phillips explains. "Gentlemen would retire to that area and smoke cigars and play cards." One night, a young man sat down to play poker. As the cards whispered across the table, his savings dwindled. "After the final hand was played, and he signed away the deed to his home, he put his pistol in his mouth and pulled the trigger."

During renovations, the poker parlors became restrooms. This unlucky spirit is now spotted in the men's room, where he recently bumped into members of a wedding party. "One of the attendees came downstairs and told our staff that he had seen someone in the men's room dressed in formal dress from the 1800s," Phillips says. According to the guest, the mysterious man looked distraught.

Although these spirits are well known, child spirits from a later era put in even more appearances at the Bourbon Orleans Hotel. "Shortly after the Civil War, this building became derelict," Phillips explains. "In 1881, it was given to the Sisters of the Holy Family, which was the first African American convent in the United States." The convent remained open from 1881 to 1963, when the building reopened as a hotel.

"The stories we most frequently hear are from the time when the sisters had it as a convent. The Sisters of the Holy Family did take in a number of orphans, and a number of them died of yellow fever." Guests often hear and see the children's spirits on the hotel's fifth and sixth floors. "People frequently report hearing children laughing," Phillips says. An employee on the sixth floor reports that the children have moved glasses on tables set for guests. "She talks to them," he says, explaining that she feels they just want some attention.

One startled sixth-floor guest has reported seeing her lavatory faucets open on their own, and many other guests see the child spirits from the courtyard. "They'll see the faces of children in the windows. Most of the reports we get are of the fifth and sixth floors," Phillips says.

This excellent hotel has 211 guest rooms, 50 of them within townhouse suites. The property also includes a full-service restaurant, a bar, and an outdoor pool. A "Haunted History Tour" departs from the lobby nightly at eight o'clock.

A Creole House is home to the ghost nicknamed Knobby.
COURTESY OF A CREOLE HOUSE

A Creole House

1013 ST. ANN STREET
NEW ORLEANS, LA 70115
504-524-8076; www.big-easy.com
$-$$$

There's a spirit afoot in this 1830s-era hotel, says manager Dave Wilson. "We don't have a bad one, but we have something in the building that's less than comforting. It's a he, and he's on the second floor." The ghost's nickname? Knobby. "He's called that because he takes off doorknobs," Wilson explains.

Wilson first saw the spirit's work in 1997, soon after he signed on with A Creole House. "I had a doorknob come off on the second floor. I asked Victor if he could replace it. About three days later, the same doorknob came off." Wilson approached the maintenance man again and asked for a *real* repair. "He said, 'You don't understand. It's Knobby.' " The maintenance man explained Knobby's mission. "I said, 'There is a ghost on the second floor that takes off doorknobs?' He said, 'Yep, he's been here for years.' "

As Wilson soon learned, Knobby averages four or five doorknobs a month. He leaves the knobs on the guest-room side of the door in place and often places the outside knobs in the hall, face down near the door. But not always. "Some days you find them, some days you don't," Wilson says philosophically.

Who was Knobby in life? An elderly neighbor claims he was the head of a family that lived in the house. "He is trying to protect his daughters," Wilson says. In many 19th-century New Orleans homes, the second floor was reserved for young women. Their parents slept nearby to protect them.

Knobby fits the pattern of a protective father. "This happen[s] on the second floor. In three years, I've never had it happen on the third floor," he says. "[And there's] always a woman or women in the room."

Females have a good chance of interacting with Knobby. "Rooms 14, 15, 16, 17, 18, 19, 20, and 21—those are the ones that seem to have the most activity," Wilson says.

Knobby once ventured to the first floor to detach the entrance doorknob. (He had already "knobbed" a couple upstairs the night before, then knobbed them again in the lobby.) Additionally, a small room on that floor is sometimes locked from the inside. An employee has also reported seeing an apparition on the third floor, in room 34. "She won't go in the room anymore," Wilson says. "I don't know if that was Knobby or not."

A Creole House encompasses three buildings. Although the greatest activity occurs in the main hotel, guests have reported sensing a benevolent spirit in room 44, in what was once the slave quarters.

Rates in this 30-room hotel include continental breakfast, a complete doorknob at bedtime, and at least half a doorknob upon rising.

Please be kind to the maintenance crew. "They're frustrated," Wilson says. "They've used glue, and screws, and Liquid Nails, and solder. They put a new doorknob in 21 three weeks ago, and it came apart in someone's hand. Whatever they do, the doorknobs still come apart."

A couple sporting Victorian clothing has been seen wandering Dauphine House.
COURTESY OF DAUPHINE HOUSE

Dauphine House

1830 DAUPHINE
NEW ORLEANS, LA 70116
504-940-0943; www.dauphinehouse.com
$

Innkeeper Karen Jeffries met the spirits in this bed-and-breakfast before she even opened for business. "My first encounter was when I first bought the house, in September of '96. We had to do a major renovation," she recalls.

Around dusk one evening, Jeffries headed upstairs to drop off some building supplies. "I was running up the stairs, and about halfway up, I was stopped dead in my tracks," she says. "It was like there was an invisible wall. I looked up at the top of the stairs, and there was this couple."

The couple sported Victorian clothing. The woman, who wore

a black dress, stood slightly taller than the man. "They were just looking at me. I remember saying that I thanked them for their lovely home, and I was going to try to restore it to its original beauty. They smiled and faded away. I dropped the stuff off really fast and left!"

Jeffries says her casual response was possibly inspired by her earlier work with a New Orleans parapsychologist. "He talked to [ghosts] this way," she says. "They are just people who, for whatever reason, are lingering."

Guests here have reported unusual experiences, too. One saw the couple on the staircase and near the sitting room. "[The guest] got the impression that they made themselves known to comfort her," Jeffries related. "Whoever they are, they seem real protective."

Another guest heard and sensed a different spirit on the balcony, says Jeffries, who's named that ghost Jimmy. "In my head, I have to imagine it's somebody like Jimmy Stewart. That's why I call him Jimmy, so I don't freak myself out," she laughs.

This bed-and-breakfast is in the French Quarter, an area known for ghosts. "The Quarter here is just incredible. Just about every inch of this area is haunted," Jeffries says. The Dauphine House was built around 1860. Its three guest rooms include microwaves, refrigerators, and coffee makers. "We're well within walking distance of everything. I'm at the end of Bourbon Street," Jeffries says.

Hotel Villa Convento

621 Urseline Street
New Orleans, LA 70116
504-522-1793
www.villaconvento.com
$-$$

Some people claim they hear children's spirits in this family-run guesthouse, but owner Lela Campo isn't sure. "I am sort of skeptical," she says.

Guests have reported hearing children on the fourth floor of the hotel, which sits on what was once part of the Ursuline Con-

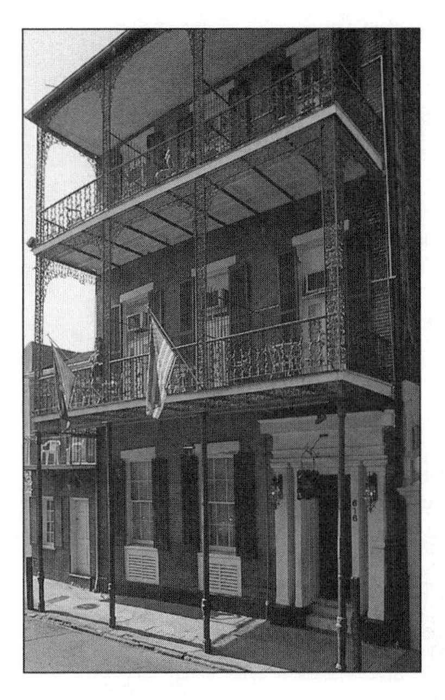

Guests at Hotel Villa Convento have reported hearing children on the fourth floor.
COURTESY OF
HOTEL VILLA CONVENTO

vent grounds. It makes sense that child spirits could be here, Campo says, because after the convent sold the property in the early 1800s, a bustling neighborhood took its place. "Sometimes children used to go play in the attics, because there wasn't much space for them to play in," she says.

Hotel Villa Convento has twenty-three rooms, plus several suites. Rates include a continental breakfast.

Lafitte Guest House

1003 BOURBON STREET
NEW ORLEANS, LA 70116
800-331-7971 OR 504-581-2678
www.lafitteguesthouse.com
$$-$$$

Several spirits linger in this elegantly restored bed-and-breakfast. "Fortunately," says innkeeper Andy Crocchiolo, "they're not mean."

Two may be the spirits of children who once lived here. "Many

The girl spirit at Lafitte Guest House has told visitors she is lonely.
COURTESY OF
LAFITTE GUEST HOUSE

people hear a baby crying," Crocchiolo says. "We also have an apparition of a young child, a little girl, and several people have seen her."

Two young visitors insist that they met the girl spirit, and that she told them she is lonely. "The two little girls brought her a rag doll, and it sits on the [dresser] now," Crocchiolo says. The lonely child's identity? "We assume it's one of the Gleises children, who died when she was about eight or ten years old in one of the yellow-fever epidemics."

An adult spirit may inhabit the house as well. Crocchiolo tells of meeting that spirit a number of years ago as he descended the interior stairs with his arms full of linens. "I started to fall, and I actually felt arms coming around my waist to pull me back. That made a believer of me."

Another time, as he and fellow innkeeper Edward Dore were planning a cruise, soot blew down the chimney into the parlor and spelled out "No Voyage" on the floor. "We went anyway, and that was the year Hurricane Betsy hit New Orleans," Crocchiolo says. He believes the spirit wanted them to protect the house during the storm.

Guests often report feeling spirits here. "Things go on and off by themselves," he says, and in suite 21, the bed sometimes moves of its own accord. Also in that room, a guest reported meeting the anguished spirit of a woman who had lost a little girl to yellow fever.

This fourteen-room inn sits in the heart of the French Quarter. Rates include a continental breakfast served in your room and a wine-and-cheese social each evening. Lafitte's Guest House also offers free, secured parking. For the best chance of meeting a spirit, ask to stay in room 21 or 22.

The Olivier House

828 Toulouse Street
New Orleans, LA 70112
504-525-8546
www.olivierhouse1.bizonthe.net
$$

Proprietors Katheryn and Jim Danner have operated this hotel for thirty years. "I have never had a personal encounter, but I have heard pretty much the same story over this thirty-year time frame," Katheryn says. "It has come from people all over the world, and so it isn't possible that the same story circulated."

Guests consistently report seeing two spirits here—a Confederate soldier and a woman wearing an antebellum gown. The woman may be former owner Elizabeth Duparc Lacoul, Katheryn says.

A friend of the Danners' is among the many guests who have seen the woman's spirit materialize in room 216. "This apparition just appeared to come out of this rippling wallpaper effect," Katheryn

Visitors at The Olivier House who have encountered its spirits have told the same story for over thirty years.
Courtesy of The Office of Community Preservation at Louisiana State University

says. "She said this female seemed to float around the room. . . . She said her mode of dress seemed to change." Eventually, the apparition faded away.

On another occasion, a guest in that same room "said he woke up, and there appeared to be a Confederate soldier and this woman in an antebellum dress standing by the fireplace," Katheryn says. "That's the story we hear very much." Some stories have the woman appearing in dresses of the early twentieth century. She is often seen clutching a rosary.

Rooms 104, 106, and 216 see the most activity. Guests also comment on odd occurrences in the Carriage House, where the bed moves on its own and the doors swing open unaided. "I have heard numerous stories from there. I think it's pretty much all over the building," Katheryn says.

Rates include parking and use of the pool.

The child spirit named Melissa died in the mid-1800s when a fire swept this site. She resurfaced when The Place d'Armes Hotel was renovated a few years ago.
COURTESY OF THE PLACE D'ARMES HOTEL

The Place d'Armes Hotel

625 ST. ANN STREET
NEW ORLEANS, LA 70116
800-366-2743 OR 504-524-4531
www.placedarmes.com
$-$$

If you see a pretty little girl strolling the fifth-floor hall of this historic inn, there are a couple of things you ought to know about her. First, her name is Melissa. Second, she's been dead around 150 years.

Melissa introduced herself to the staff a few years ago during the hotel's restoration, says Warren Valentino, an owner and the general manager of the Place d'Armes Hotel. "When we renovated this building, we did it by floor," he says. "As we did each floor, we sealed off the floor that was being renovated so people wouldn't be in danger. It was nailed closed very securely every night."

The trouble began when the work reached the fifth floor. The switchboard operator received an unexpected call. "The switchboard indicated that room 508 was trying to check the front desk," Valentino says. The problem? The fifth floor's electricity and phones had been disconnected.

To make sure no one had wandered into the construction area, the desk clerk headed upstairs. Finding the entrances to the fifth floor boarded up, he shrugged the call off. "We figured it was the phone system," Valentino says.

"About a week later, the same thing happened, and it was reported again. The third time it happened, we were concerned that there was an electrical short in that area."

They sent an electrician up. "The guy undid the plywood from the door at the opposite end of the building and looked toward 508, at the end of the hall," Valentino says. "In the doorway was what he described as a twelve-year-old girl in a First Communion white lace dress. [She was] standing and staring at him." The electrician fled.

"We got concerned," Valentino says. "So we started to do some research."

What he learned danced shivers along his spine. A huge fire swept through this section of New Orleans in the mid-1800s. "The building on this site caught fire," Valentino says. "There was a mother and daughter who lived on this site, and the child was lost in the smoke of the fire, and died in the fire. She was described in the newspaper here as a twelve-year-old." Her name? Melissa. "It was definitely this address, and we know this is exactly the lot. It fits perfectly with the tragedy that happened here a long time ago."

Melissa may appear "anywhere on the fifth floor," he says, but she seems most at home near room 508. "My theory is that's the place she died in, and it's about where her spirit remains. That's where we'll get a housekeeper saying that she walked past that entranceway and felt a temperature change." Interestingly, Melissa has never been seen inside room 508, only in the doorway and hall.

"We have an occasional guest who comes down and talks about a little girl that they saw on the fifth floor," Valentino says. "We just say we'll look into it. [These are] people who have never been here, who give us clues that confirm that there is a situation here that nobody much wants to talk about."

The Place d'Armes Hotel includes seventy-eight guest rooms, a courtyard, and a pool. Adjoining valet parking is available. Rates include continental breakfast and a morning newspaper.

You'll want a room on the fifth floor, of course. "I can no longer write it off," Valentino says. "Something's there."

Three antebellum structures make up the Prytania Inns
COURTESY OF THE PRYTANIA INNS

The Prytania Inns
The McGuinnes Mansion

2127 PRYTANIA STREET
NEW ORLEANS, LA 70130
504-566-1515
www.thebestofusa.com/prytania
$

Three antebellum structures make up the Prytania Inns, and two of them are noted for their ghost stories. Of the inns, it's the McGuinnes Mansion that sees the most activity, according to front desk clerk Ulysses Marrero, a ten-year employee.

Which room is most active? Marrero pinpoints room 9, which is visited by a "woman in white."

"The first incident I can remember involved a German woman with a four-year-old son," he reports. "She called me, hysterical, and told me that her child kept looking over her shoulder and screaming, 'Look at the white woman!' "

Several months later, two young women called Marrero to room 9. "They called me one night and complained about a chair sliding back and forth in the little foyer attached to the room," he recalls. Marrero went to investigate. "While climbing the stairs to the second floor, [I] heard the chair sliding. Hoping to catch them in the prank, I opened the door. The chair immediately stopped sliding. The two girls were on the bed, clinging to one another in horror."

A third incident involved a long-term resident also staying in room 9. She had often seen a tall woman dressed in white at the top of the stairs, but the woman always left by the time the tenant reached the spot.

The tenant assumed the woman in white was another guest and didn't give her much thought until, one night, she almost caught up with her. The woman in white turned the corner and dematerialized.

The shocked tenant entered her own room—room 9. "Before she could turn the light on, [she] saw a glow in the corner of the room and turned to find herself face to face with the 'white woman,' " Marrero notes.

This inn is located five minutes from the French Quarter by street car; ten to fifteen minutes by foot. Rates include a full Southern breakfast. Of course, you want to request room 9.

The Prytania Inns
St. Vincent's Guest House

1507 Magazine Street
New Orleans, LA 70130
540-566-1515
www.thebestofusa.com/prytania
$

St. Vincent's Guest House, at 1507 Magazine Street, is the second haunted structure associated with the Prytania Inns. St. Vincent's began life as an orphanage, and some of its lost children still play here, Marrero says.

St. Vincent's was built in the 1860s by Margaret Haughery, an orphan who lost her own child to yellow fever, subsequently dedicated her life to easing other children's suffering. Hundreds of chil-

St. Vincent's Guest House was built by Margaret Haughery who dedicated her life to easing the suffering of orphans.
COURTESY OF ST. VINCENT'S GUEST HOUSE

dren passed through the orphanage. Although many went on to better lives, some died here of yellow fever.

Guests report hearing these children's spirits running in the halls, and employees have been annoyed by children giggling at them from "behind the walls." They have also spotted the form of a nun on the top floor of the second wing.

St. Vincent's Guest House is a ten- to twenty-minute walk from the French Quarter. Rates include a full Southern breakfast, access to pool and courtyard, and free on-site parking.

ST. FRANCISVILLE

Myrtles Plantation

Please see the feature on page 3.

The spirits of a mother and daughter, who were murdered in the 1890s, linger at Bienvenue House.
COURTESY OF BIENVENUE HOUSE

Bienvenue House

421 NORTH MAIN STREET
ST. MARTINVILLE, LA 70582
888-394-9100 OR 337-394-9100
www.bienvenuehouse.com
$

Leslie Leonpacher, the innkeeper here since 1996, suspects two spirits may linger in this bed-and-breakfast. "In the late 1890s, a mother and daughter were murdered here," she says.

In 1896, the year of the murders, travelers knew this inn as the Evangeline Hotel. Innkeeper Isabell Robertson and her two daughters—one an invalid, one a toddler—were home the night the killer broke in. Only the toddler escaped alive.

Former owners reported hearing the older girl, who was bedridden, ring a bell for help. "They would hear bells ringing in the night," Leonpacher says. One guest has reported that small objects move in the room where the girl died.

When the home was being renovated, workers' radios turned on and off without visible cause. Leonpacher suspects that Isabell Robertson was trying to get the workers to skedaddle. "I do feel as if Isabell is a very friendly spirit, if anything. I don't feel any animosity from her," she says.

This bed-and-breakfast is on the National Register of Historic Places. Rates include a full gourmet breakfast and a welcome tray. The child spirit is most active in the Josephine Room.

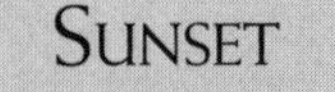

Chretien Point Plantation Bed-and-Breakfast

665 CHRETIEN POINT ROAD
SUNSET, LA 70584
800-880-7050 OR 337-662-5876
wwwvirtualcities.com
$$-$$$

"Our ghost story started during the War of 1812," says Louis Cornay, who owns and operates this historic bed-and-breakfast with his wife, Jeanne. "The man who built this house was a young man at the time."

Like many area planters, Hypolite Chretien marched off to war in 1815 as ten thousand British troops bore down on the undefended city of New Orleans. "Andrew Jackson was in Florida," Louis says. "He came tearing over from the Panhandle of Florida with about two thousand [soldiers]." The famed Louisiana pirate Jean Lafitte joined forces with Jackson, adding his thousand pirates to the army. "And then the planters and their sons were there," Louis says.

During the battle, a fellow American fell near Chretien, who left the safety of his trench to offer aid. "Chretien pulled him to

The ghost of a pirate shot by Felicite Chretien still haunts the plantation.
COURTESY OF CHRETIAN POINT PLANTATION BED-AND-BREAKFAST

safety and bound up his wound," Louis says. "They introduced themselves to each other. . . . The other man said he was Jean Lafitte, the pirate."

After the war, when Lafitte could no longer safely sell his goods in New Orleans, Chretien became his partner, which added to Chretien's fortune. "The pirates did real well, as well," Louis says.

Jean Lafitte died in 1826 and Chretien a few years later, but trade continued. "Felicite Chretien was Louisiana's first liberated woman," Louis chuckles. "She took over the reins of the plantation when her husband died, and she continued to deal with the pirates."

Those dealings soured in 1840, when the buccaneers decided to head west. "They needed some money," he says. "So they came one night to rob this house. Felicite was alone with her children."

One of the band entered the house and snuck up the stairs. Felicite heard him coming. She grabbed her pistol and a handful of jewelry and stationed herself at the top of the staircase. When the pirate saw her and hesitated, she rattled her jewels to draw him near. Up the stairs he climbed. "When he got close enough, she pulled the pistol from behind the skirt. She shot him in the head," Louis says.

As the other pirates fled, she and her slave stashed the body in the cupboard under the stairs. They cleaned the carpet but not the wood underneath. "There is a bloodstain on the stairs still, to this day," Louis says.

There's also a seafaring son of a gun under the stairs.

"When we first moved here, I had absolutely no belief in ghosts." But, Louis says, "every time we would have a tour and I would make fun of these ghosts, we had major electrical problems."

The first time he scorned the ghost, somebody (or something) leaned on his car horn outside. Louis went out to disconnect the horn but instinctively waved his hand over it instead, as if pushing a hand away. "It stopped," he says. "That happened twice. A few months later, in another tour, I made fun of the ghost, and this time, he just honked the horn on my car and kept on until I stopped."

His tours no longer slur the pirate, whom the Cornays call Robert.

Other spirits—including possibly the Chretien children—share the house. "We've heard children playing in the parlor upstairs, and whispered conversations," Louis says. Guests and staff have reported chairs rocking on their own in the children's old room, as well as doors unlatching and opening themselves. One guest reported seeing a dense fog in the house and simultaneously hearing children playing jump rope. "It's all very innocent," he says.

Then there are the soldiers, he says, noting that a Civil War battle raged on these grounds. One evening, Louis and Jeanne heard three men talking at the foot of the stairway. Louis investigated but found the house empty and the doors locked. Soon afterward, a guest told them that his great-grandfather, a photographer during the Civil War, had once photographed three officers at the foot of the same stairs.

This twelve-room mansion is furnished with antiques. It offers five guest rooms. When the Cornays bought it in 1975, it was furnished with hay; farmers had converted it into a barn. "The house was built in 1831, . . . ahead of the plantation houses up and down the Mississippi," Louis says. "The style of this house is the basis for the construction and style of all the other ones. The stairway in this house was copied by Hollywood for Tara" in *Gone With the Wind*.

The grounds include flower gardens, tennis courts, and a pool. Rates include a mansion tour, a full plantation breakfast, and mint juleps in the evening.

Please don't scoff at Robert the pirate and his fellow spirits. "As long as you let them know that you acknowledge their reality, they're okay," Louis says.

VACHERIE

Oak Alley Plantation

3645 LA 8
VACHERIE, LA 70090
800-44ALLEY OR 225-265-2151
oakalleyplantation.com
$-$$$

Tour guide Petesy Dugas has good reason to believe spirits occupy this antebellum mansion. One tossed a candlestick at her not too long ago.

On that particular day, Dugas led her tour group into the dining room. "There were two tall, slim candles set on this little table," she says. "And as the tour group was walking in, one of the candles fell on the floor. I just thought it was the vibrations [from people walking]."

A visitor put the candle back in its holder. "I closed the doors," Dugas recalls. She then took her place across the room and began

The Lady in Black strolls the majestic oak allee at Oak Alley.
COURTESY OF LOUISIANA OFFICE OF TOURISM

her speech. "I was about two or three minutes into my talk. I was facing the candle. All of a sudden, that candle—it didn't just fall out, it *flew* halfway across the room. I wouldn't believe it if I didn't see it."

She looked at the thirty-five stunned members of her tour group. "Everybody was sitting there with their mouths open," she laughs.

Realizing the group would take its cue from her, Dugas teasingly addressed the thrower. "I said, 'Okay, we'll keep our voices down.' " She went on with her speech, joking that the group couldn't visit the third floor because "that's where the ghosts are."

Dugas still doesn't know who threw the candlestick.

Two spirits claim center stage at Oak Alley.

First, there's owner Josephine Stewart, who died here in 1972. "[People] have seen her in the windows," says director of sales and marketing Donna Oliver. Employees report that she flips lights off and on. She may also fiddle with the clocks, which were stopped at the time of her death.

Then there's the Lady in Black. This spirit, who strolls the majestic oak allee, once posed for a photograph. The photo, snapped in a bedroom in the mansion, shows a young woman sitting before a mirror. "She is wearing an antebellum costume," Oliver says. "You can't see her face, but you can see her long, black, wavy hair." The mirror reflects the room behind her—but not the lady herself. The photo is on display at Oak Alley.

Some think the Lady in Black is Louise Ramon, whose father built the house. "People have seen her out on the balcony and throughout the house," Oliver says.

And then there's the little stuff.

Employees have reported seeing empty rocking chairs rock and hearing horse-drawn carriages clip-clop up the gravel drive. A guest reported seeing the ghosts of three men fighting on a balcony. Some people hear a child cry. Others see ghostly figures sitting on the beds and standing in the kitchen. The lights routinely flicker when one guide gives tours, though they remain constant for other guides.

Speaking of lights, Petesy Dugas remembers the day she and fifteen tourists heard something fall in an off-limits side room. They peeked around the corner. "It looked like somebody had lit up a Christmas tree with clear lights," she reports. By the time her manager arrived, the form had disappeared. "There was not even a place to plug lights" in the room, she says. Still, sixteen people saw those lights. "It's hard to explain. . . . Before I came here, I never thought about ghosts," she says.

She definitely thinks about them now.

You can't spend the night in Oak Alley's "Big House," but the grounds include five early twentieth-century Creole cottages without televisions or phones. Children are welcome. Rates include a full country breakfast. Guests can tour the mansion for a fee.

MISSISSIPPI

Vicksburg, the scene of a fierce Civil War battle and prolonged siege, harbors more spirit activity than any other city in Mississippi. But King's Tavern in Natchez may offer the best chance to rub elbows with a ghost.

King's Tavern

619 Jefferson Street
Natchez, MS 39121
601-446-8845
www.kingstavern.com

Madeline and Friends

King's Tavern owner Yvonne Scott can flat-out tell some ghost stories. Drop by for dinner and she'll give you the lowdown on the hundreds of sightings connected with this historic property. Then she'll tell you what she knows for a fact. "I will swear to what I've seen," she says. And Scott's seen plenty.

King's Tavern, the oldest building in Natchez, opened its doors sometime before 1789, operating as a stage stop on the Natchez Trace. Aaron Burr and Andrew Jackson dropped by; so did the outlaw Big Harpe, who did his damnedest to add to the ghost population.

Today's "regulars" include an assortment of ghosts: a young woman named Madeline, a baby, and a man in a top hat. Scott, who bought the inn in 1995, sensed a presence here before she saw one. "When we first got it, I was in there cleaning one day, and I was going back into the restaurant," she recalls. "I took about three steps inside the restaurant, and I am telling you, the hair just stood up on the back of my neck, and I just stopped dead. Have you ever heard the expression 'frozen with fear?' I actually froze, and I was thinking, 'God, what is *this*?' Something just scared me to death, it really did. I looked, and I saw nothing whatsoever. When I could move, . . . I backed back through the doors.

"To this day, I've never had that experience again," she says. "Whatever it was, I am telling you: I did not belong in there at that point in time." Though Scott always looks for a logical explanation for the things that happen in this inn, she can't always find one. One day, for instance, an employee watched a woman's footprints track across his just-mopped floor. No woman—just prints. "He saw the footsteps coming toward him. He took off running and never came back," laughs Scott, who also saw the prints. "They were small, like a small woman's footsteps." The woman walked barefoot.

"I tend to think, 'Well, okay, it could have been somebody that had varnished the floor, and maybe somebody walked on it, and the prints came through. . . . But I've tried to get the footsteps back, and I never could.' "

Whose footprints were they? Madeline's, perhaps.

Ricardo King, who operated the inn until 1817, had a mistress named Madeline. According to legend, the distinctly unamused Mrs. King murdered sixteen-year-old Madeline one night and bricked her body up in the fireplace.

Death barely slowed Madeline down. Employees say she knocks jars off shelves, pours water on the floor, turns lights on, breaks glasses, turns water on and off, and sashays about the tavern. "My daughter one time saw Madeline in front of the fireplace," Scott adds.

Scott has never seen Madeline, but she's been in her presence. In one area, chains decorate the tavern walls. One day, Scott and a visitor were sitting nearby discussing Madeline. "A chain started swinging back and forth. I was sitting by the chain and it did—I swear to you—it started swinging. And I was thinking, 'Uh, this is really weird,' " she says.

Madeline, the murdered mistress of a former owner of the tavern, is still a presence today.
COURTESY OF KING'S TAVERN

Again, Scott looked for a logical explanation; again, she struck out. "We have gone upstairs and jumped and tried to make [the chain] move. It will not move unless you touch it," she says. "It really did just start swinging, and I'm thinking, '*Jeez*.' "

Several folks have reported seeing other spirits here, too. "I have always heard about a man that is here," Scott says. "They always called him 'the Man in the Top Hat.' A lot of the waitresses have said he is the evil one.

"I had never seen this person until a year ago. Again, I was by myself in the building. I had just come out of the restroom. There stood this man. And he stood there, and I looked at him, and he was gone, just like that. He had on a top hat, a dark jacket, and pants. I think, and I am not real sure about this, but in my mind I can even see this black string tie."

She has also glimpsed a male apparition by the tavern fireplace.

King's Tavern, the oldest building in Natchez, opened its doors sometime before 1789.
COURTESY OF HISTORIC NATCHEZ ON THE MISSISSIPPI CONVENTION AND VISITORS BUREAU

One day, four visitors posed for a photo there. "My little granddaughter said, 'Who is that person standing there?' I had already seen him. There was a spirit behind them. . . . But whatever it was, and it was a spirit of some sort, didn't come out in the picture."

His proximity to the fireplace may not bode well for him. He may have shared Madeline's fate.

In the 1930s, the Pilgrimage Garden Club of Natchez bought the building to save it from destruction. During repairs, workers discovered a grim surprise in a bricked-up fireplace. "There were three skeletons in there," Scott says. One was a sixteen-year-old female—Madeline. The other two were males. Although some people claim workers found a jeweled dagger buried in Madeline's breast, that isn't so, according to Scott. "The dagger was in another fireplace, in another room. When they were renovating the building, the dagger fell out of the fireplace in the tack room."

How did three bodies wind up in the fireplace? If the spirits know, they aren't talking.

Though rumors of other spirits float about the tavern, Scott has personally experienced only one more: a baby.

"They say that one of the Harpe brothers had been in here," she says, referring to the band of outlaws. Legend says a mother and her baby were staying in the attic room when the baby's cries annoyed Big Harpe. "He picked the baby up by its feet and slung it against the fireplace and killed it," she says. The baby's wails come from the attic when the door is opened. "I have heard the baby cry, but I haven't heard it in four or five or six years," she says. "It's really been very quiet up there."

King's Tavern isn't a bed-and-breakfast, but if you've ever wanted a chance to spend the night alone in a haunted house, this may be it. "I do let people occasionally stay up there—the ghost chasers, I call them," she says. "Sometimes they get an experience, and sometimes they do not."

Drop by for dinner and talk to Scott. A note of warning, though: once she locks the doors, she's going home. "When they're there, they're really on their own," she says.

GREENWOOD

Rivers' Inn

1109 RIVER ROAD
GREENWOOD, MS 38930
662-453-5432
$

Rose Marie Kennedy bought this bed-and-breakfast in December 1991. Before the new year rolled in, she knew she had a ghost.

"I had only been living here just a few nights," Kennedy says. "All of a sudden, I heard clanging and breaking noises. It sounded like somebody was tearing out all the plumbing in the bathroom."

The noises moved to another room. "I heard what sounded like someone dragging a piece of furniture across the room. Then the noise seemed to change locations," she says.

She tracked the noises to the kitchen. "It sounded like a tray of silverware being moved across the counter and falling on the floor.

Noises at Rivers' Inn move from room to room.
COURTESY OF THE RIVERS' INN BED & BREAKFAST

I was so petrified then that I thought, 'I am going to call the police,' but I couldn't because I was too scared to let them in. Eventually, it stopped. I didn't hear it anymore for several nights."

The noises—silverware falling to the floor in the kitchen, someone dropping the corner of the dresser in the room next door, an unknown object somersaulting down the stairs—have often returned.

"Nobody else ever hears it," she adds. "It's never happened when somebody else was in that bedroom. Maybe the ghost is just a private person, a private spirit. Periodically, I still hear the scraping of silverware across the countertop and then a few pieces falling on the floor."

Rates here include breakfast and access to the courtyard and pool. "My main business is catering, so I do a wonderful full breakfast—raspberry pancakes, sour cream eggs," Kennedy says. She serves evening appetizers and keeps the place well stocked with mint iced tea.

When you stay here, request a downstairs room.

King's Tavern. Please see the feature on page 39.

Heavy, deliberate footsteps were heard upstairs in Monmouth Plantation.
COURTESY OF SYLVIA HIGGINBOTHAM

Monmouth Plantation

36 MELROSE AVENUE
NATCHEZ, MS 39120
800-828-4531 OR 601-442-5852
www.monmouthplantation.com
$$-$$$

When Lani and Ron Riches bought this historic Mississippi plantation house on Valentine's Day in 1977, they had no idea a ghost came with it.

Like many innkeepers, they realized the house contained an interested spirit when they began renovations. "We were really in restoration mode," Lani says. "And Ronnie and our dear friend . . . who helped us greatly with the interior design, both were standing in the hall, and they heard footsteps." The heavy, deliberate footsteps were upstairs. "They even called the police another time. They thought somebody was here. . . . The footsteps were way high, in the attic. It was those heavy, heavy footsteps." The house was empty both times.

"And then my children, before the house was finished, they woke up hysterical, hearing the footsteps. . . . I never have had the experience," Lani adds. "It's been my husband, my children, and workers." On each occasion, more than one person heard the steps.

The Riches assume the footsteps were those of John Anthony Quitman, a Mississippi governor and cotton baron who lived here until the 1850s. It's possible that the former United States congressman was curious about the Californians moving into his home.

In any event, the spirit has settled down. "We have anointed every part of this house and prayed over it," says Lani. She believes the spirit may have been calmed by the quality of the restoration as well. "We think that he got happy," she laughs. "I think it probably looks better than when he lived here."

Monmouth Plantation has sixteen suites and fifteen guest rooms, many with working fireplaces. It has received a Four-Diamond rating from AAA and is home to an excellent gourmet restaurant. The landscaped grounds include a croquet lawn, a short hiking trail, fishing ponds, and tennis courts. Rates include a full Southern breakfast and evening hors d'oeuvres.

Pass Christian

Harbour Oaks Inn

126 West Scenic Drive
Pass Christian, MS 39571
800-452-9399 or 228-452-9399
$-$$

Innkeepers Tony and Dianne Brugger kicked their raucous spirit-houseguests out years ago, but they believe the spirit of a helpful child remains behind.

The spirit of a helpful child remains at Harbour Oaks Inn.
COURTESY OF HARBOUR OAKS INN

"Our inn is the only nineteenth-century inn on the Mississippi coast," Tony says. The antebellum hotel was commandeered as a hospital during the Civil War. Several spirits, possibly of soldiers who died here, inhabited the house when the Bruggers began renovations several years ago.

"It was one area upstairs that the fellows stayed in," Diane says. "My only tangible experience is whenever I would go up to the second floor, I would feel this crushing feeling on my chest, and my hair would just raise on end. I had to force myself over the threshold."

"They were unruly," Tony adds. "They were not happy people." In fact, the innkeepers finally had to give their guests the heave-ho. "We had a sensitive come in and ask them to leave."

"And then there's the little girl," Tony says. "She stays in the first floor here, and pretty much stays in one room. We call it the Red Room. When we bought this place, it was painted bright, bright, bright red."

Although many guests sense this spirit, one couple had a particularly dramatic run-in with her. "The night before, my daughter, who was working as a waitress, was missing a button on her tuxedo-type uniform. No matter where we looked, we couldn't find any black thread or buttons in the house," Tony says. The next morning, a couple staying in the Red Room asked if the inn had ghosts. "When I asked these people what had happened, they said they heard noises and turned on the lights. Twice. The third time, there was a rather loud crash, and they turned on the lights, and on the floor was an antique sewing case with nothing [in it] but some black thread and black buttons. They knew nothing about what happened to us the night before. Only bad thing was that they kept the case," he laughs.

"I do believe my daughter has seen the spirit," he says. "I think she's about twelve years old or so, and possibly mildly retarded. . . . I think it's possibly the same little girl who frequents a couple of doors down," he says, referring to a local restaurant. "They've had the same thing, except it's in the wine cellar. They go down there, and there are bottles all over the floor."

"We've had guests experience her. . . . As soon as they realized there was something in the room, then the sense would vanish, and they were disappointed," Diane says. This spirit has been quiet recently. "I have a feeling it's because my daughter grew up and moved out," she says. "[The spirit] is quite a pleasant little thing, and she is very helpful. We think the little girl is still around here. She's just very quiet now."

A sensitive has told the Bruggers that the child's mother hovers in the background. In the nineteenth century, Pass Christian was a popular vacation spot. New Orleans aristocrats summered here to escape the fevers that swept through the city. Diane feels the mother and child may have brought the fever with them and died here.

This beautiful old inn is listed on the National Register of Historic Places. It offers a beach view and is furnished with antiques.

The Bruggers say you have the best chance of making the spirit's acquaintance in the foyer, the sitting parlor, and the two rooms on the east side of the house.

Vicksburg

Vicksburg, the scene of a decisive Civil War battle, is well known for its ghosts.

While you're in town, you may want to visit the battleground and the museum known as the McRaven House. "They're crawling with ghosts," says innkeeper Bill Smollen of the 1902–08 Stained Glass Manor–Oak Hall.

Anchuca's ghost pulls up a chair and sits by the fireplace in the dining room.
Courtesy of Anchuca Bed-and-Breakfast

Anchuca Bed-and-Breakfast

1010 First East
Vicksburg, MS 39183
888-686-0111 or 601-661-0111
$-$$

Pay special attention to the dining room of this Greek Revival inn, which dates to around 1830. According to local legend, that's where you're most likely to see the spirit of a young woman.

"The ghost story is that supposedly there was a man that lived here, who had a daughter," says innkeeper Loveta Byrne. "And she was dating this guy that he did not want her to date. He refused to let her date him anymore, and so she wouldn't eat. She'd sit by the fireplace, and that's where she stayed."

People very occasionally glimpse the young woman today. "The people that owned this house saw the ghost in the dining room. She'd pulled up a chair by the fireplace," Byrne says. "I have not had any experience with the ghost. The only thing I have felt was approximately two months ago. I felt a presence which was startling. I have had guests in the slave quarter tell me that they feel like there is a ghost in there, but I have not experienced that."

Confederate States president Jefferson Davis made a speech from the balcony of this house, which is listed on the National Register of Historic Places. Rates include a full Southern breakfast and a tour of the property. The main house has two guest rooms furnished with antiques and heirlooms; connected properties include other accommodations. The amenities include a pool and a Jacuzzi.

Cedar Grove Inn

220 Oak Street
Vicksburg, MS 39180
800-862-1300 or 601-636-1300
www.cedargroveinn.com
$$

You can't get much more Southern than Cedar Grove Inn. "It's Greek Revival, and just as you always think about the Southern mansion with the big columns. . . . It has wonderful verandas and porches," says owner Estelle Mackey.

It even claims a souvenir from the Civil War. "It has a cannonball embedded in the parlor wall," Mackey says. It seems that Elizabeth Klein, who lived here during the war, kept the cannonball as a memento. "The reason that it wasn't taken out after the war by the Kleins was that Mrs. Klein was a relative of William Sherman," she explains.

A relative of William T. Sherman's living in Vicksburg?

One of the spirits at Cedar Grove Inn smokes a pipe in the gentleman's parlor.
COURTESY OF CEDAR GROVE INN

"This was a true North-and-South home," Mackey explains. John Alexander Klein hailed from Virginia. "He was a Southern gentleman. He was not only a cotton man, a lumberman, an architect, a jeweler. . . . He was everything." Elizabeth's family, on the other hand, hailed from Ohio. "Her family migrated to New Orleans when she was fourteen. They met when she was fifteen, and he waited a year to marry her. She was sixteen, and he was thirty." They married in 1842. John gave Elizabeth Cedar Grove Hall as a wedding gift.

During the war, John fought for the South. Elizabeth was pregnant during the siege of Vicksburg, and Sherman, her kinsmen, had her moved behind Union lines to make sure she delivered her baby safely. Elizabeth appreciated the gesture. "She named [the baby] William Tecumseh Sherman Klein," Mackey says.

By the time Estelle Mackey and her husband, Ted, bought Cedar Grove in 1983, the old home had fallen on hard times. "It was really kind of sad when we purchased it," she says. "It wasn't in grand condition. We had to do a lot of work on the grounds. We bought back the old carriage house that was out of the family and just put everything back the way it should be. . . . Then we purchased homes across the street and turned them into . . . cottages, and they are part of the inn. So, today, we sit on five acres." The cottage John Alexander Klein lived in while building Cedar Grove is now a honeymoon cottage.

Two spirits inhabit the house.

Mr. Klein checks out visitors. "He used to smoke a pipe," Mackey says. "In our gentleman's parlor, if he doesn't feel like he's liking whoever's sitting around in there, all of a sudden you start smelling the pipe."

The other spirit is a young girl. Several family graves were moved when the property changed hands in 1919. "Since that time, there has been a young girl who walks the steps of Cedar Grove," Mackey says. "She's very restless and is only seen by people who really believe in ghosts." But both believers and nonbelievers hear her on the stairs. "You can hear her sometimes, creaking on the steps. In fact, one night, we had guests that were staying right by the steps, and they couldn't sleep all night. They said, 'We heard walking on the steps, but we couldn't see anything.' "

Cedar Grove Inn's accommodations include guest rooms in the main house and several historic cottages. "Of course, breakfast is included with the stay," Estelle says. "In the afternoon, we have complimentary tea, and it's served in a beautiful wicker garden room overlooking the grounds. We also have an award-winning restaurant in the mansion." The chef specializes in "a blend of French and Southern cooking." Also on the grounds are an antique shop, a gift shop, a chapel, and a small collection of antique cars.

When you make reservations, ask to stay on the mansion's second floor. If you believe in ghosts, peek outside when you hear the child spirit wandering. "They say that she's a pretty little girl with long hair, and she looks like she's sad and lost."

1902–08 *Stained Glass Manor–Oak Hall*

2430 Drummond Street
Vicksburg, MS 39108
800-771-8893 or 601-638-8893
www.vickbnb.com
$-$$

Some innkeepers keep mum about their ghosts. Not Bill and Shirley Smollen. They tell folks up front that they might meet a ghost in this historic house. The Smollens decided some time ago that they might as well. "The ghosts were making so much noise, they were keeping the guests awake," Bill explains.

Guests here have frequently reported hearing voices singing nineteenth-century tunes, doors opening and closing, lights turning on and off, and someone making "oddball noises." "This was before we had the place exorcised in 1996 or 1997," Bill says.

The exorcism toned things down, but one spirit slipped through. "That was Fannie, the lady who built the house. She has never been a noisy ghost."

The Smollens, who bought the inn in 1995, didn't know they'd claimed a houseful of ghosts. Bill first suspected something was up when certain items began disappearing and then reappearing. For example, his twenty-five-foot tape measures constantly went AWOL. "We couldn't find them to save our soul," he says. "You couldn't find a camera to take a picture, and then *all* of them would come back. Numerous things were gone. We get some of that [activity] periodically now, but it's not as frequent and certainly not as noticeable."

These days, guests most often report seeing or sensing a presence the Smollens identify as Fannie Vick, a philanthropist who lived here until 1931. "Five people have actually seen her. Four have felt her presence but have not seen her. Everybody who has seen Fannie has had a [prior] out-of-body experience," Bill says. "You know—you died, you saw the white light, and then somebody brought you back."

Those who have seen Fannie describe her as a woman with

Fannie Vick Willis Johnson, the lady who built 1902–08 Stained Glass Manor—Oak Hall, survived the house's exorcism.
COURTESY OF 1902–08 STAINED GLASS MANOR-OAK HALL

long brown hair, wearing a white robe. The Smollens say they aren't sure how many people have actually had an experience with her. "For every one that tells us, we figure three don't," Bill says.

One of the people who "met" Fannie reported a remarkable effect. A couple reserved Fannie's Room. The wife was grieving a family tragedy. Her husband went down to check on their luggage. "According to [the wife], somebody came over, and she felt it was feminine," Bill says. The woman reported feeling "like someone had given her a warm, warm hug." She said she felt that whoever hugged her "took the grief upon themselves. By the time her husband got back with the luggage, she was over it," Bill says, referring to the wife's grief. "They finally related the experience three days later. It shook her up pretty bad. She didn't see her, she just felt her."

The Smollens often welcome tour groups to this Mission-style home, which is listed on the National Register of Historic Places and is noted for its stained-glass windows.

"I've had grown men come to the door [of Fannie's Room] and couldn't walk in the room. I'd later in the tour ask them if they had nearly died [at some point in their lives], and they'd say yes," Bill says. "We have had a number of children touring the house. They

This photograph shows orbs floating in Fannie's former room.
COURTESY OF 1902–08 STAINED GLASS MANOR-OAK HALL

will not go into the room. They will go in and come straight out." It's unclear whether these guests are reacting to Fannie or to other energies that investigators and guests have photographed in the room.

"I am the most cold-blooded engineer you ever saw in your life," says Bill, a former systems engineer for NASA. "I don't believe in these things. But when I see things appear on film, and my buddies at Kodak or Polaroid can't explain it, then I've got to shift my mind and [my] thinking on it. I think what convinced me was the photographs—things showing up on photos where you don't see them with the eyeball. It's independent of film; it's independent of film and camera type. It ends up being some sort of energy form that shows up on film or on the digital image."

Many of those photos show orbs floating through or around the house. "In one photo, here's Fannie's Room, and there must be seventy-five or a hundred orbs in it," Bill says. "It was taken by a tourist who mailed us five or six photographs that they took while they were in the house. . . . The fascinating part about the orbs and the energy images is they do not show up in every photograph in sequence. Let's say you're taking photos seven seconds apart. The energy shows up on only one out of three, one out of four images."

One set of investigators used a magnetometer to measure the electromagnetic impulses in the rooms. "The magnetometer went berserk in Fannie's Room and one other place," Bill reports. "There used to be a servant's quarters or nursery up on the third floor. [The magnetometer] reacted as [the investigator] approached the door to the attic. . . . It's as if there were some traumatic or some emotional event, [and] those emotions elevated the energy levels."

As for Fannie, she was most recently seen on the inn's lawn. "The thing about Fannie's ghost is she's never scared anybody," Bill says. "She's very, very loving. This is a loving friend."

Expect a pleasant experience at this beautifully restored inn, which includes six guest rooms and a cottage. Ask to stay in Fannie's Room. And bring a digital camera.

ALABAMA

Alabama claims only a handful of haunted inns—fewer, in fact, than any other Southeastern state. You'll find its most famous haunted bed-and-breakfast, Grace Hall, in Selma.

Grace Hall

506 Lauderdale Street
Selma, AL 36701
334-875-5744
www.traveldata.com
$

Miss Eliza and Barney Doolittle

Visitors have spotted four ghosts in this 1857 mansion, according to owner Coy Dillon—five, if you count the dog.

Miss Eliza, the primary ghost-in-residence, first turned up in 1982. Coy and Joey Dillon accidentally photographed her standing in an upstairs window. "But logic took over, and we dismissed it as a shadow or sunlight," Coy explains.

Three small children spotted her next. They asked the Dillons about the beautiful lady in the long white gown, and about her small black dog.

The puzzled innkeepers did a little research. They found that after the Civil War, Anna Evans turned Grace Hall, the former mayor's residence, into a boardinghouse. She ran it with the help of a black man named Pappy King. Anna soon invited her niece, Eliza Jones, to move in, too.

The Dillons identified the apparition as "Miss Eliza" Jones, who

The two spirits who haunt Grace Hall are Eliza Jones who lived here from 1878 to 1940 and her dog, Barney Doolittle.
COURTESY OF GRACE HALL

lived here from 1878 to 1940. The pooch? It's her dog, Barney Doolittle, who rarely left her side.

Since then, Miss Eliza has been a frequent guest, mostly when young ladies or small children visit. Miss Eliza had four daughters, which could explain the attachment.

Although guests frequently saw her, Coy Dillon didn't meet Miss Eliza until 1996. Around daylight one morning, he spied her strolling across his side porch. "She came from where the courtyard is, up the stairs, and then around the kitchen, and was going down to the front side of the building when I saw her. And she was probably no more than maybe fifteen feet from me. The form was so distinct that I thought possibly one of my guests had gotten up and was out on the porch," he says. "When I turned the light on, there was nothing there."

Guests have identified several other spirits at Grace Hall. They include Anna Evans, her employee Pappy King, and the spirit of Mr. Satterfield, who lived here until 1923.

A stay in Miss Eliza's house includes a full breakfast, afternoon

Miss Eliza was first photographed standing in an upstairs window at Grace Hall in 1982. At right is a detail of the window from the photograph above.
COURTESY OF GRACE HALL

beverages and snacks, and a guided tour of the mansion, which is listed on the National Register of Historic Places and features a thousand square feet of porches. The grounds include a walled garden.

The ghosts at Grace Hall like to entertain; they are most likely to appear when the house bustles. "It's always been when there are a number of people here and a number of young people, or young ladies. That seems to be an enticement for them. This was a very social family all of their life," Coy says.

Miss Eliza would probably like to know that Grace Hall welcomes children age six and over; Barney Doolittle welcomes pets by prior arrangement.

Part of the medical staff from the building's former days is still on duty at the Pickwick Hotel.
COURTESY OF PICKWICK HOTEL AND CONFERENCE CENTER

Pickwick Hotel and Conference Center

1023 TWENTIETH STREET SOUTH
BIRMINGHAM, AL 35205
205-933-9555
www.pickwickhotel.com
$-$$

"From what we can tell, this building used to be a medical arts building," says Pickwick's former director of sales, Chris Champion. "It was built in 1931, and it had doctors' and dentists' offices in it." The Art Deco building was renovated in the mid-1980s and reopened as a hotel.

Part of the medical staff may still be on duty.

Many people believe a nurse who once worked here haunts the hotel. No one knows who the nurse was in life, but rumor has it she died in an auto accident. "They say that she came back to the building, and she's on the eighth floor," Champion says. As far as she knows, no one has seen the nurse. "I will say that the elevator does go up to the eighth floor unexpectedly sometimes."

Guests at this sixty-three-room hotel are welcome to draw their own conclusions. "We don't charge extra to stay on the eighth floor," Champion laughs.

ELBA

Aunt B's Bed-and-Breakfast

717 WEST DAVIS STREET
ELBA, AL 36323
877-621-5894 OR 334-897-6918
www.bbonline.com/al/auntbs
$

Patti Brooks didn't realize this old home was haunted until she began operating it as a bed-and-breakfast in 1999. "This is my grandparents' house, and it was built in 1910 by a young doctor and his family in this little town," says Brooks, a minister. "My grandparents bought the house in 1914 and lived here until my grandmother died in 1967."

Aunt B's sits on the site of a former Federal Civil War prison.
COURTESY OF AUNT B'S BED-AND-BREAKFAST

Another set of owners turned the house into a bed-and-breakfast. Brooks bought it in 1999, taking a back room for her quarters. That room, an enclosed porch, has several windows and a sliding glass door leading outside. "I had been here a couple of weeks when, about five in the morning, my little dog started growling, and it woke me up. . . . And I look at the window, and I saw a man with a ponytail. He had a screwdriver, and I could see his wrist turning." The man was trying to remove the window screen, she says. Brooks called 911, but the police search came up empty.

Over the next weeks, she was awakened several times by people trying to jimmy the same window. "There's a big security light in the backyard and venetian blinds on the window, so you see the silhouette of whoever is outside. I called the police a minimum of twice a week, sometimes twice a night, with various people looking in the window." The figures always disappeared before police arrived. "I will tell you, you will doubt your sanity after a while," she says.

Finally, Brooks began to suspect her guests were ghosts. Some research bolstered her theory. She learned her house sat on the site of a Federal Civil War prison. "There was a garrison here," she says. "I [became] convinced that these men were soldiers. I think they were trying to get into the infirmary."

She also determined that her back room sits over a huge artesian well. "There is this big tunnel of water," she says. She feels the energy from the water's flow may have something to do with the apparitions.

Although the first figures at the window were males, women and children soon began to arrive. One night around eleven o'clock, she says, "I woke up and there was a child standing at the patio door. I thought, 'I am going to have to get up and see about this.' " She initially believed the child had wandered away from a neighborhood party. "I got up and walked over to the door. There was a little girl out there, and she had on high-button shoes with a little nightgown that came below her knees." When she saw the shoes, Brooks knew the child was out of time. "I knew that was a ghost, and so I came back to bed."

Believing the apparitions were spirits in need of direction, Brooks decided to help them. The next night, she awakened to find a woman and a two-year-old standing in her room. "Within a couple of nights, I had another woman." One night, she found a child leaning against her bed. "I woke up with a little Down syndrome child, with her chin on her hands, looking at me." Each time, Brooks said, " 'Do you see the light? I know you see it. Go on to the light.' As soon as I'd say it, they'd start to pull in and fade away." Some nights, she says, as many as seven spirits materialized in her room.

Traffic has now slowed. "It seems to have abated somewhat," Brooks says. "I don't know if the backlog is unclogged or what."

This bed-and-breakfast has three guest rooms. Rates include a Southern breakfast. Brooks doesn't normally mention the ghosts. "Several guests have asked me if I have any ghosts, and I tell them what I think they can handle," she says.

If you'd like to stay in the back room, just ask. Brooks will gladly accommodate you.

PRATTVILLE

Rocky Mount Bed-and-Breakfast

2364 ROCKY MOUNT ROAD
PRATTVILLE, AL 36033
800-646-3831
$

Sharron Cobb, who owns and operates this 1891 bed-and-breakfast with her husband, Jim, doesn't know exactly who haunts the small room at the end of the hallway, but she figures it's a member of the family. "This is a family home," Sharron explains. "My husband's great-grandfather built this house. His grandmother was born and raised here, his father was born and raised here, and then he grew up across the road."

This spirit loves music, which has helped the Cobbs narrow the list of suspects. Topping that list? Great-Aunt Mae. "Jim's

The spirit of Great-Aunt Mae, who is the woman standing on the left in this family photo, still roams Rocky Mount.
COURTESY OF ROCKY MOUNT BED-AND-BREAKFAST

great-aunt Mae . . . was engaged, and we're not sure what happened to the engagement, but the engagement was broken off, and she died a spinster. After the marriage was broken off, she would go to a church maybe an eighth of a mile [away] in the middle of the night, in her pajamas, and play the piano. And her father would go down there in the middle of the night and get her and bring her home."

The music-loving spirit often visits a small hallway adjacent to the dining room. "I keep my CD player there with piano music for the guests' breakfast," Sharron explains. "It just started coming on sporadically. There was no set time to it. It didn't come on every day or every other day or once a week. It was sporadically." Over the years, the Cobbs have often caught a whiff of sulfur in the area. They believe it may be connected to the spirit. "It's only in that particular room," Sharron says.

Others have also sensed a presence in the house. "We had a woman here helping with a wedding, and we had never mentioned [the spirit] to her, and she looked at my husband and said, 'You know you have a ghost, don't you?' " The woman had been in the same hallway cutting and arranging flowers. "She said her scissors were moved. And she went on to say she felt the presence of there being a ghost."

The Cobbs restored this family home in 1982. "We lived in [the house] not quite 17 years, and then we opened the bed-and-breakfast in February of 1999," Sharron says.

The bed-and-breakfast contains two guest rooms. Rates include a full country breakfast. For a fee, guests can ride the horses in the pasture.

SELMA

Grace Hall. Please see the feature on page 57.

St. James Hotel

1200 WATER AVENUE
SELMA, AL 36701
800-678-8946 OR 334-872-3234
www.nthp.org/main/hotels/alabama2.htm
$-$$

Unlike many Southern ghosts, the spirits in the meticulously restored 1837 St. James Hotel have nothing to do with the Civil War. "One's a female by the name of Lucinda. She's believed to be the ladylove of Jesse James," says general manager John Jewett. Another may be Jesse James himself.

Visitors associate Jesse and Frank James with the Old West, but the outlaws liked to kick back in this riverfront establishment. "Jesse James used to vacation in this hotel," Jewett says. "The whole band did."

One of the ghosts who resides in St. James Hotel is reported to be the ladylove of Jesse James.
COURTESY OF ST. JAMES HOTEL

Lucinda may have actually lived here. "The hotel back then was more of a tavern for which people could occupy a whole room, so the guest rooms were like long-term rentals, like apartments," Jewett explains. "Guests have seen Lucinda in suite 214. She's tall, with black hair. . . . There's a picture of her in our lobby. She was very attractive."

She seems to be a calm presence. "She's walking around," says Jewett. "She's going about her business. We've had people come down very shaken because they think that she does [talk to them]. For the most part, people say she merely looks at them." Some guests say she wears a lavender scent. "She's seen sometimes in the bar, just drifting through," he adds.

A dog's spirit also romps around the second floor of this no-pets-allowed hotel. "The dog has not been seen, but he barks. I've not heard him, but I was here in the hotel when somebody called [asking us] to get the dog quieted down." Whenever guests complain about the barking, staff members say they'll check into it at once—and do. But there are never any dogs to be found.

Although you might guess the dog is protecting Lucinda, Jewett doesn't think so. "More speculation is that it's Jesse's," he says.

Guests and staff sometimes spot a male spirit upstairs and in the bar. "You'll see him in adjacent sleeping areas up there. He's been seen up on the third floor. People see him coming from a guest room—214, 314, 315." The jangle of his spurs draws people's attention, he explains.

Why do people think it's Jesse? "It's the costuming," Jewett says. "He wears Western clothes.

"My own experience on a personal basis is hearing glasses rattle behind the bar, and seeing them moving, and not seeing anything [to move them]. We have a long bar, and these glasses were stacked up on the back. . . . [An employee] yelled at him to stop messing with the glasses." The glasses stopped moving at once.

Ask for Jesse's table when you visit. "He likes the table in the corner, to the left of the bar and mantel," Jewett says. Some employees have seen him there. Others have reported seeing "fleeting shadows" throughout the hotel or being touched by spirits.

The St. James Hotel, which recently underwent a $6 million restoration, includes forty-two guest rooms, four riverfront suites with balconies, and a gift shop. Its Troupe House Restaurant specializes in regional cuisine.

FLORIDA

St. Augustine claims more haunted inns than any other city in Florida, but St. Petersburg Beach hosts the state's most famous haunted hotel. At the Don CeSar Beach Resort and Spa, founder Thomas Rowe still strolls among his guests more than a half-century after his death.

Don CeSar Beach Resort and Spa

3400 Gulf Boulevard
St. Petersburg Beach, FL 33706
800-637-7200 or 813-360-1881
www.don-cesar.com
$$$

The Dapper Mr. Rowe

One sunny afternoon not long ago, a new employee of the Don CeSar Beach Resort headed for the resort's seven-mile beach, hoping to catch a little sun. She and her husband spread their blanket and settled in. She scanned the sandy shore and the Gulf of Mexico's gently lapping waves. As the gulls wheeled overhead, she felt someone in the distance gazing at her. "She noticed a man in a light-colored suit and a Panama hat, looking very dapper," says Susan Armstrong, director of guest services. "It kind of tickled her."

The woman nudged her husband. "She said, 'Look at that guy. He looks like Panama Jack,' " Armstrong says. Her husband sat up.

Left: Thomas Rowe, who always dresses in a light-colored suit and Panama hat, still takes care of business at the resort he founded.

Below: Thomas Rowe built "The Don" as a Taj Mahal to a lost love.

COURTESY OF DON CESAR BEACH RESORT AND SPA

He looked up the beach. He looked down the beach. "He said, 'What guy?' "

The gentleman had disappeared. "He literally vanished into thin air," Armstrong says. "She didn't think anything of it at the time, because she didn't know anything about Thomas Rowe at the time."

She soon found out.

The dapper Thomas Rowe, who always dresses in the light-colored suit and Panama hat, died here in 1940, but that hasn't stopped him from quietly taking care of business at the fashionable resort he founded. He chats with workers, checks out new employees, warns of danger, and gently corrects guests who speak harshly of his hotel.

He has good reason to be protective of the resort known simply as "The Don," says Mary Ellen di Pietra, who leads the resort's haunted history tour each October. "Thomas built this as a Taj Mahal to a lost love," she says.

Rowe's love story opens in the early 1920s, when Rowe visited Italy and fell passionately in love with a young opera star named

Lucinda. He proposed. Lucinda said yes, but her parents said no, believing a marriage would ruin Lucinda's future in the opera.

Rowe returned to the United States brokenhearted. His health soon crumbled as well. His doctor ordered a move to Florida.

If Rowe's doctor had rest in mind, he was sadly disappointed. Rowe, a real-estate man, bought eighty acres of land for a resort hotel and drew up plans for a Moorish-flavored castle. The hammers started flying. He named his three-hundred-room "Pink Palace" the Don CeSar, after a character from his favorite opera. "The opera was called *The Maritana*. The main character was Don Caesar. Everything here is named for the opera," says di Pietra, who is also the hotel's small-wedding coordinator.

The Don opened in 1928 but faltered when the stock market crashed. As Rowe continued welcoming his influential guests, including F. Scott Fitzgerald and FDR, his health slowly ebbed. Ironically, his doctor prescribed "medicated cigarettes," hoping their menthol would heal him. It didn't. Rowe died here, in the hotel he loved, in 1940.

The first clue that he hadn't really checked out? The cigarettes. "Employees used to smell the menthol in places he frequented," Armstrong says.

Employees didn't have long to track him. A year after Rowe collapsed, the hotel's finances followed suit. With war on the horizon, The Don slipped into military uniform. The United States Army bought it for a fraction of its original cost, enlisting it for use as a hospital and rest-and-relaxation post. "There were reports of sightings of ghosts then," Armstrong says, though no one thought to record them.

The Don entered the postwar years as a drab government building. By the early 1970s, the once opulent "Pink Palace" faced the wrecking ball. Fortunately, history-minded citizens intervened. The Don underwent an extensive renovation beginning in 1973.

Rowe's interest in the property apparently underwent a restoration as well. A dapper gentleman in a light suit and a Panama hat soon became a regular on the construction site. "He would question the crews as to how things were going," Armstrong says. The builders checked out his wardrobe and figured him for ho-

Don CeSar was named after a character in Rowe's favorite opera.
COURTESY OF DON CESAR BEACH RESORT AND SPA

tel administration. They politely answered his questions, keeping him up to date on their progress. "That was Thomas Rowe," she chuckles.

Usually, Rowe maintains a low profile. In fact, he's entered a guest's room only once.

A photographer had come to do a shoot for a popular magazine. She arrived the day before and spent the night at the hotel. The next morning, she went to the public relations office demanding to know if The Don had a ghost. "She said, 'I saw a man in my room last night, and he spoke to me. He kept telling me, "Don't let her sit on the ledge," ' " Armstrong says.

What did he look like? The photographer sketched the face of her midnight guest. "It was an absolute match for Thomas Rowe," Armstrong says, adding that no photos of Rowe were displayed in the hotel at that time.

Rowe's meaning became clear during the shoot. The photographer had planned to have a model perch on the ledge of the penthouse patio. But as she set up the shot, she remembered Rowe's warning. "She went over and examined [the ledge], and it was quite crumbly," Armstrong says. "Thomas Rowe saved the model's life."

Rowe has also been known to interact with guests who "speak harshly about the hotel in his presence," according to Armstrong. While less civil spirits might hurl glasses or fling silverware, Thomas Rowe still practices restraint. For instance, guests recently criticized The Don in the resort's florist shop. "All of the flowers in the cooler kind of collapsed," Armstrong says. In another case, he tugged at a woman's skirt until she fell silent. "They could see her skirt standing away from the body," she laughs.

By the way, Thomas Rowe isn't the only spirit walking The Don's halls. People also see a female spirit here, possibly a World War II nurse. They report seeing a woman with "short, dark, kind of curly, old-fashioned-style hair," di Pietra says. "And the hat and the uniform are old fashioned. People give the same description of her. We'll have the same story repeated."

Guests say she exits a supply closet carrying linens and other supplies. But in fact, there is no supply closet. "She may materialize as if she's coming out of a wall," Armstrong says. Guests and employees often spy the nurse on the ground floor near the spa. "One sighting was in a walk-in freezer. [The employee] turned around and saw her face in the little square window."

No one knows who this woman is or why she's working overtime. Some people think she had an attachment to Rowe. Others think she had a wartime romance with a soldier who passed through these doors.

This beautifully restored hotel has 277 guest rooms, plus restaurants, ice cream parlors, gardens, pools, and a white-sand beach that lazes along the Gulf of Mexico. It is listed on the National Register of Historic Places and has received a Four-Diamond rating from AAA. Nearby attractions include the Salvador Dali Museum and Busch Gardens.

"We do a history tour throughout the year on Wednesday and Saturday, and we get into the ghosts if people want to," di Pietra says.

Keep an eye open for Thomas Rowe. Little things happen throughout the hotel. "Lights come on, televisions go on and off, the music goes up and down," di Pietra says. "That's fairly frequent."

"Rowe appears on the first floor, which is where he passed away, and up on the fifth floor, which is the other public area of the hotel," Armstrong adds. "Anytime there's any construction going on anywhere in the hotel, whether it's [building] or painting, he materializes in those areas."

The Island Hotel and Restaurant today
COURTESY OF ISLAND HOTEL AND RESTAURANT

CEDAR KEY

Island Hotel and Restaurant

373 SECOND STREET
P.O. BOX 460
CEDAR KEY, FL 32625
800-432-4640 OR 352-543-5111
www.islandhotel-cedarkey.com
$-$$

Several spirits roam this 1859 inn, says innkeeper Tony Cousins, who has operated it with his wife, Dawn, since 1996.

For starters, employees and guests report seeing the spirit of an old woman in the downstairs lobby. "She doesn't do anything. She's just dressed in old-fashioned garb. And when you ask her what she wants, she disappears," Tony says, adding that her clothes date from the late 1800s or early 1900s.

"There is another lady upstairs," he says. "Guests have woken up during the night and seen her sitting on the end of their bed, looking at them. And when challenged, she gets up and walks off, and she'll walk through walls and out of the room."

Dawn Cousins has glimpsed a tall, dark, bearded man upstairs—possibly the spirit of Simon Fienberg, who was murdered here in 1918.

"Florida still had Prohibition in 1918. It was still a dry state. Fienberg owned the hotel and had a manager here," Tony says. During a surprise inspection, Fienberg found that his manager was operating a still in the attic. "He got quite upset. The manager, to show there was no hard feeling, put on a sumptuous meal for this Simon Fienberg, during which he poisoned him. He retired to bed and never woke up. . . . He has relatives who still call about him, to see if anyone has seen him."

Former innkeeper Betsy Gibbs still visits the hotel, too. "She owned the hotel from 1948 to 1973. She was the lady that really put the hotel on the map, and made it famous in Florida," Tony says. "She moves things. I put tools down, and when I come to pick them up, they're gone. She's mischievous. If you want to do things she doesn't like, they don't come about. If she approves, things

Betsy Gibbs, seen here with her husband, is still a mischievous presence at the inn.
COURTESY OF ISLAND HOTEL AND RESTAURANT

Several spirits roam the Island Hotel and Restaurant, which was built in 1859.
COURTESY OF ISLAND HOTEL AND RESTAURANT

get done. She's very influential like that. Betsy's perfume will linger," he adds.

According to legend, the spirit of a child may haunt the basement. The child hasn't been seen, but Tony says he sometimes senses the boy's spirit—or scares himself into thinking he does. "There are . . . times that I can't go down there at all, but if I do, I've got to go out," he says.

"And then the last two are in the annex." The annex, like the main inn, was built in 1859. "There is apparently a little girl in one of the rooms in the annex. Guests see her. She's just there and then disappears." A second spirit snores in another annex room. "It is a very definite human snore. We've heard it several times," Tony says.

This inn, listed on the National Register of Historic Places, first served as a general store and post office. It includes a well-known seafood restaurant and The Neptune Bar, a popular local watering hole. People come here for quiet, among other things; the guest rooms do not have phones or televisions.

The ghost who resides in The Grady House likes to play chess.
Courtesy of The Grady House

High Springs

The Grady House

420 NW First Avenue
High Springs, FL 32643
904-454-2206
www.gradyhouse.com
$-$$

Innkeeper Kirk Eppenstein makes no bones about it. "We definitely have a ghost," he says. "Neither Tony nor I were big believers in the supernatural before we got here, but now we're definitely believers in ghosts."

Eppenstein and Tony Boothby didn't realize this two-story Arts and Crafts–style house was haunted when they bought it in 1998. But it didn't take the resident spirit long to introduce herself to Eppenstein. She got his attention via a one-sided game of chess.

"There is a chessboard in the end of the hallway upstairs," Eppenstein says. "The first thing that I noticed was the pieces kept being moved." The first time it happened, he thought a guest had tinkered with it. "There was one piece moved to a certain square, and another piece placed on top of it," he says. He put the pieces right. But he soon realized that someone was making the same move over and over as guests came and went. "I would be the only person here taking care of everything, and the same thing would happen, time and time again.

"A short time later, Tony and I were in the house and heard footsteps in a room above us, where there weren't any guests. In fact, the house was empty except for us. We heard footsteps going back and forth. And it wasn't too long after that that a guest was awakened by someone walking back and forth in that same room," he says.

Guests began mentioning strange experiences in other rooms, too. "In one room, guests report over and over again that they are awakened in the middle of the night by an extremely sweet smell, like lilacs or orange blossoms. In a different room, we have had several guests say that they felt someone tucking them in at night. Again, they were a little bit startled, but they didn't feel alarmed. They felt comforted.

"And then I have one room where a woman has actually appeared. She was in a nightgown, a very conservative nightgown from previous times," Eppenstein says, noting that the gown had a high collar. "She was grooming her hair in the mirror and then disappeared. The guest felt startled but not alarmed, and was able to fall right back asleep."

As for the chess game, it continued until Eppenstein simply had enough of it. "We had a lot of activity until I went upstairs by myself and the chess pieces were moved, and I said out loud, 'Okay, I know you're here. Knock it off.' Since then, it only happens sporadically."

Eppenstein says most guests walk right by the chessboard without realizing anything is amiss. The one exception came the time Tony's uncle paid a visit to The Grady House. Eppenstein told the uncle about the activity but didn't describe the spirit's signature move. The uncle "thought it would be fun to scare his wife and move the chess pieces," Eppenstein says. But when he got up to look at the board, the spirit had put them back in the signature position—one piece on top of the other. The uncle "came down the next morning for breakfast, and he was white as a sheet," Eppenstein laughs. The move didn't surprise Eppenstein. "When people challenge her, right after that, we will have a series of events," he says.

The innkeepers have no idea who the spunky spirit was in life, since many people lived in this former boardinghouse. "The people that lived here have never been able to associate any kind of tragedy with the house," Eppenstein says.

The Grady House, which is listed on the National Register of Historic Places, includes five guest rooms and a cottage. Rates include a full hot breakfast, as well as cookies and lemonade in the afternoon. Guests receive complimentary wine in their rooms.

Visitors enjoy tubing, canoeing, and kayaking on the local rivers. "We have the highest concentration of freshwater springs in the world," Eppenstein says. "Jenny Springs is world-famous for cave diving."

When you visit, you may want to ask for the Red Room, where the spirit has twice materialized. "She's tucked people in [in the Red Room] three times," Eppenstein says. "The Peach Room is always where the perfume is. And then she always walks in the Green Room.

"I've never lived with a ghost that I've known of, but I don't feel the least uncomfortable. In fact, it makes me feel protected," he says. "We feel like she's kind of watching over the house. She's a very nurturing spirit."

Of course, he's doing his part to nurture her, too. "We have a collection of old 78s and a Victrola, and I will sometimes play an old song for her," he says. "I think she likes Ella Fitzgerald."

Beyond her love for jazz, Eppenstein knows only one thing about this spirit: She is no Bobby Fischer. "She obviously doesn't know how to play chess, the way the pieces are moved," he says.

Artist House

534 EATON STREET
KEY WEST, FL 33040
800-582-7882 OR 305-296-3977
www.artisthousekeywest.com
$-$$$ (SEASONAL)

Michael Wright, co-owner of the Artist House since 1998, doesn't think the inn is haunted. "But that's immaterial," he says. "Many people do."

The Artist House's ghost story enjoys a long history. It revolves around artist Robert Eugene Otto, whose father built the home in the late 1800s. "Gene was born here in 1900," Wright says. "When he was a boy, seven or eight years old, his Bahamian 'mammy' gave him a life-size doll as a birthday gift. Now, she was supposedly a voodoo priestess—no one knows," he adds quickly. But that's the story.

"Gene named the doll Robert and took [the name] Eugene for himself. Throughout his life, whenever anything bad happened, Eugene blamed the doll."

Eugene studied art at the Academy of Fine Arts in Chicago and in Paris, where he met musician Annette Parker. They married in 1930 and eventually came home to this house in Key West. Throughout their life together, "Robert was sort of his alter ego—his evil twin," Wright says. "Theoretically, Anne used to lock the doll away in the turret, and the doll would reappear. Whether it was evil, etc., etc.—I really wouldn't know."

The doll is gone now, on display at the East Martello Museum in Key West. Even so, some people say a spirit remains. "It's argued that Anne, after she passed away, would appear in the house, and there are those who claim to have seen her," Wright says.

Some guests still claim to "see things" in the house. "The former owner of this place really played up that angle," he says. "I don't. I think it's a question of you see what you want to see."

The Artist House is a well-known Key West landmark featured

on local ghost tours. Many people believe it to be haunted. If you'd like to draw your own conclusions, you'll find yourself in pleasant surroundings.

This bed-and-breakfast, one of the most photographed buildings in Key West, has seven guest rooms and serves an expanded continental breakfast. No children, please.

Two little girls who have been seen at Eaton Lodge may be the twin daughters who lived here in the late 1800s.
COURTESY OF EATON LODGE

Eaton Lodge

511 EATON STREET
KEY WEST, FL 33040
800-294-2170 OR 305-292-2170
www.eatonlodge.com
$-$$

For years, innkeeper Carolyn West didn't know whose spirits rambled around her lodge. "Different guests have said they have heard footsteps, and seen a shadow go past [beneath their door]. They go to open the door, and they fling the door open, and nobody's there," says West, who bought the lodge in 1995.

One guest reported meeting an entire family. "She said a woman in a formal dress, a man in an old-fashioned suit, and two little girls kept them up all night," West says.

One spirit's creative frenzies at an unseen typewriter inspire even more questions. "I have had many guests come down and ask me,

'Who's typing at night?' Obviously, people [now] have PCs and not typewriters. People don't even *type* on typewriters anymore."

West solved all of the home's mysteries when the great-grandson of a former owner dropped by. He told West that his ancestor, Dr. William Warren, pounded out speeches on typewriters. That solves the mystery of the clacking typewriter. "We're assuming it's the doctor," she says. He also told West that a family with twin daughters lived here in the late 1800s, which explains the second set of ghosts.

West hasn't seen any spirits here, but she has heard someone upstairs. "It was a pacing sort of movement, enough to make an innkeeper wonder, 'What is that maid *doing* up there?' " When she investigated, she found the room locked and empty.

"Then, of course, you have the usual lights that switch off and now they're on, and this is missing and now it's here. This is standard. Throughout the years, I've had many guests say the exact same things."

Built in 1886, Eaton Lodge is listed on the National Register of Historic Homes. The compound includes Eaton Lodge, two other historic buildings, and a garden. Rates include an island breakfast and a hospitality bar; amenities include a pool and a whirlpool spa.

For the best chance of encountering spirits, request a room on the second floor.

MICANOPY

Herlong Mansion Bed-and-Breakfast Inn

402 NW CHOLAKKA BOULEVARD
MICANOPY, FL 32667
800-437-5664 OR 352-466-3322
www.herlong.com
$-$$

You have the best chance of meeting this bed-and-breakfast's spirit in Mae's Room. "I'm sure we have had over a thousand

Guests at Herlong Mansion are invited to guess which room is the "ghost's room."
COURTESY OF HERLONG MANSION

instances in that room," says former owner Sonny Howard. "We've had a few in other rooms, but 90 percent or more have been in Mae's Room."

Guests have reported seeing apparitions floating through the room, hearing doors open and close, and sensing a presence. Researchers have identified unusual electromagnetic energies in the room as well.

Howard began the tradition of offering tours of the house and inviting visitors to guess which room is the "ghost's room," a tradition current owners Julia and Lon Boggs continue. "Consistently, at least half of the people who guess will guess Mae's Room," Howard says. "You ask them why, they'll say, 'I feel energy in that room' or 'The temperature is different.'

"I have heard the door to that room open and close on two occasions," he adds. "Both times, I was on the phone, thinking nobody was here. And when I go up and check, there *wasn't* anybody here."

Howard believes the spirit is former owner Inez Herlong, who died in the house. "She had gone through this eighteen-year family

Guests consistently guess that Mae's Room is the "ghost room" because it feels different.
COURTESY OF HERLONG MANSION

fight to get it," he says. "And the day she took possession, she died here of a heart attack, by herself." Her nemesis in the legal feud was her kinswoman Mae, who lived in what is now known as Mae's Room for twenty years.

Julia and Lon Boggs bought the inn in November 2000. Lon had what may have been his first experience with Inez only a few days after the purchase. "There's a thermostat right beside Mae's Room," he says. "I went up to check the temperature on the thermostat. It was pretty warm and humid here. . . . I moved the thermostat, and I turned to walk away, and I got chill bumps all over. I could feel the hair on the back of my arms and the back of my neck stand up."

This house, built in 1845, was modified to its current Southern Colonial Revival style in 1910. It has eleven rooms, suites, and cottages. Rates include a full Southern gourmet breakfast. Children are welcome.

St. Augustine

Although many people think of Jamestown, Virginia, as America's first permanent European settlement, St. Augustine predates Jamestown by forty-two years and Plymouth Rock, Massachusetts, by fifty-five. It is, in fact, the oldest permanent European settlement in North America—and one of the most haunted.

Founded by Don Pedro Menendez de Aviles in 1565, the city first represented Spain's interests in the New World. Florida achieved statehood in 1845, and in the 1880s, St. Augustine became a fashionable winter resort. Today, historic St. Augustine remains an impressive, and well-ghosted, destination.

If you're looking for a ghost tour in St. Augustine, try Tour St. Augustine, Inc. Call 800-797-3778 or 352-825-0087.

Casa Blanca Inn Bed-and-Breakfast

24 Avenida Menendez
St. Augustine, FL 32084
800-826-2626 or 904-829-0928
www.casablancainn.com
$-$$

There's a ghostly legend associated with this place, but according to manager Audrey Mather, no one's recently reported any activity within the inn itself. "Not that I'm aware of," she says, "and I've been here three years now."

The legend actually places the inn's ghost on the roof of the building.

It seems that during Prohibition, rumrunners routinely sailed into the bay. The Casa Blanca Inn, then known as the Matanzas Hotel, profited handsomely from the illegal trade. When the federal authorities zeroed in on the property, the inn's owner signaled her rumrunning friends from the rooftop, waving a lantern to warn them away.

Neighbors and mariners still see her lantern swaying from the

Casa Blanca's ghost resides on the roof of the building.
COURTESY OF CASA BLANCA INN BED-AND-BREAKFAST

rooftop. Some people also report seeing a dark figure on the roof.

Rates at this historic inn include breakfast and complimentary beverages.

Casa de la Paz

22 AVENIDA MENENDEZ
ST. AUGUSTINE, FL 32084
800-929-2915 OR 904-829-2915
www.casadelapaz.com
$-$$

The spirit in this historic bed-and-breakfast has a fondness for music boxes, says Donna Marriott, who formerly owned and operated the inn with her husband, Bob.

"I collect music boxes, and I have probably about fifty out in the living room," Donna says. The spirit played all but one: an electric carousel. "The night that we plugged that in, the power went off in the living room three times. . . . I got the feeling that she was trying to tell us that she didn't like that one, that she didn't want this new stuff."

Guests have also had unusual experiences in the front bedroom,

The spirit in Casa de la Paz has a fondness for music boxes.
COURTESY OF CASA DE LA PAZ

the Ponce de Leon. "Probably the most common [report] is a sensation that there is somebody in the room with them. We've had a few guests say they just kept looking over their shoulder, that it felt as if somebody was with them." Other guests report the television flashing on and off all night.

One guest described "a feeling of water on her neck," says Donna. She didn't know what the woman meant until she felt it herself. "I was sleeping on our sofa one night. And I woke up and felt like there was water on my neck. A few weeks later, [Bob] was in our bed, and the same thing happened to him. It's just an eerie sensation. The best I can figure is ghosts do things with electrical impulses that just feel wet. There's definitely no water there. It's always the back of the neck."

The Marriotts assume the spirit is female for two reasons.

"Supposedly, the people that renovated this house back in the eighties were giving a grand-opening-type party," Donna says. "At that time, supposedly, someone saw this young lady coming down the stairs."

The second reason? A sweet odor sometimes precedes the presence. "It is just really pleasant," Donna says. One guest described the fragrance as "something that smelled like her grandmother used to," she adds. "It's almost a comfort now that I know what it is. I say, 'Oh, she's in here with me. I can't see her, but she's here.' "

Casa de la Paz has six guest rooms and serves a full breakfast. It also offers wine in the afternoon.

Ask to stay in the Ponce de Leon, the room with a ghost and a view. "The room that we feel her the most in probably has the best view of the bay of any room in St. Augustine," Donna says.

St. Francis Inn

279 St. George Street
St. Augustine, FL 32084
904-824-6068
www.stfrancisinn.com
$-$$

The St. Francis Inn's ghost story revolves around two eighteenth-century lovers, says assistant manager Beverly Lonergan, who's met them both.

"Lily was a slave girl here," Lonergan explains. "Lily had a love affair with, we think, the nephew of one of the many owners that owned the inn. We don't know his name, but they had a love affair going on, and they used to meet up on the third floor. . . .

"The nephew was a soldier. The story is that she got pregnant, and the family, for whatever reason, wouldn't let it happen. We have many different versions of this story. The story that we really think happened is that she killed herself, with the baby. Another story we were told is that they paid her to go away. But we figure it was the first story, they were so in love.

"I've seen Lily," Lonergan adds. "I haven't seen her face, but I've seen the back of her on the second floor. It was busy one day, and we had a girl that worked here named Connie. And her son had called, and I ran up to the second floor to get her."

In the second-story hallway, a small woman rushed past. "I thought it was Connie that whizzed by me. I said, 'Connie?' There

The St. Francis Inn's ghost story revolves around two eighteenth-century lovers.
Courtesy of St. Francis Inn

was dead silence, and the hair on the back of my arm stood up."

She remembers the apparition clearly. "She had black hair—very coarse black hair—and she was very tiny. She was carrying something, and I couldn't see if it was towels or a baby." The woman didn't remind her of a servant. "She was dressed too clean to serve."

Connie, as it turned out, was in another section of the house at the time.

"I've also seen the soldier," Lonergan says. "I've seen him on the downstairs level. I'll never forget this. I was doing my paperwork, and it was quarter after ten, and there wasn't a soul around. I felt movement in the side of my eye, and I turned around and looked, and he was just leaning against the doorway, very comical, with his arms crossed and smiling.

"Boom, he was gone.

"What he had on was dark blue britches, and he had the kind of hat that points in the front and a red jacket on with shiny brass buttons. He was really dressed up nice. Very handsome." According to historians, that uniform may have been worn by colonial militiamen from St. Augustine or Cuba.

Lily once spoke to Lonergan and a fellow worker in Anna's Room, located on the second floor. "I heard a very slight whisper hello," Lonergan says. "I said, 'Did you hear that?' And [the worker] said, 'I sure did.' And she ran out of the room, and I ran with her," she laughs.

Guests often report experiences, too. "We do have many people that come down and say, 'What's going on up in Lily's Room?' " The television goes on and off on its own. "One lady felt a kiss on the cheek in the middle of the night," Lonergan says. "We had a lady that felt her feet were being touched. We've had this quite a bit: we've had people say that they had a pocketbook dumped and the makeup explored." Lipsticks, especially, disappear.

Models often come here for photo shoots. "This is the oldest continually running bed-and-breakfast in St. Augustine," she says, noting that the inn is listed on the National Register of Historic Places. "We have a drop-dead beautiful courtyard. A lot of photographers bring their models." In one case, the models stayed in the second-floor suite where Longeran saw Lily. "We had a horrible rainstorm. They decided to go out to lunch. They came back, and [a model] went up to her room, and she came downstairs, and she said, 'Bev, somebody was in my makeup.' She says, 'I know I closed it. But what I'm really upset about is the rain came through the window. Not a drop of the rain went in the case, but it was all around.'"

The St. Francis Inn is located in the heart of St. Augustine Antigua. Built in 1791 of coquina limestone, the inn includes a courtyard and a lush garden of tropical plants—banana trees, bougainvillea, and jasmine, among others. The inn has twelve rooms and suites, some with refrigerators or kitchenettes. Rates include a full breakfast, use of the inn's bicycles, and a social hour.

When you visit, ask for Lily's Room, Anna's Room, or Elizabeth's Suite (which contains Anna's Room). You may want to leave some lipsticks out—and to keep your eye open for a small, dark-haired woman and her handsome lover.

St. Petersburg Beach

Don CeSar Beach Resort and Spa. Please see the feature on page 68.

GEORGIA

Most of Georgia's ghosts cling to the old cities and towns along the coast. Savannah hosts more ghosts than any other city, but a resort on Jekyll Island harbors a trio of spirits—two on timeless vacations, one eternally on the job.

Jekyll Island Club Hotel

371 Riverview Drive
Jekyll Island, GA 31527
800-333-3333 or 912-635-2600
$$$

Barons and Bellhops—Paradise on Hold

September 4, 1886. On tiny Jekyll Island, a barrier island off Georgia's southern coast, the paint brushes and cleaning rags are flying. The new Jekyll Island Club, with its magnificent Queen Anne clubhouse, opens in four months. There are windows to wash, floors to buff, chandeliers to polish. Behind the clubhouse, a cluster of servants' quarter stands beneath the pines. Vacation "cottages" will soon go up along the sound-side drive, providing winter getaways for America's wealthiest families. In fact, the club's membership will eventually represent one-fifth of the world's entire wealth. Vanderbilts, Astors, Morgans, Pulitzers—everybody who is anybody will meet here.

As workers race to finish their tasks, a skiff makes its way from the mainland, across the sound. The news it carries flies around the island: Club president Lloyd Aspinwall is dead!

"Lloyd Aspinwall was really a very popular person," says Sue

The Jekyll Island Club, with its magnificent Queen Anne clubhouse, opened in 1886.
COURTESY OF JEKYLL ISLAND CLUB HOTEL

Andersson, director of guest services for Jekyll Island Club Hotel. "He was highly respected. And he was very much caught up in the club and how it was going to happen."

How involved was he? As it turns out, Aspinwall may not have missed the club's opening at all. His friends spotted him several times in the club's earliest days, in a glassed-in section of the veranda now known as the Aspinwall Room. In fact, he's been seen off and on for the last century. Most recently, a guest "saw a visage of an individual described as with military bearing—mutton chops, and *very* good looking," Andersson says. "He passed into view and then out of view." The guest asked the staff why they had a man in costume on the veranda.

Aspinwall isn't the only club member who didn't let death cancel his membership. Samuel Spenser, once the president of the Southern Railroad Company, still reads his paper in The Annex. "Spenser did, indeed, have a second-floor apartment, and he really did enjoy it," Andersson says.

Spenser and his wife often vacationed here in the early 1900s. His death in 1906 was both tragic and ironic. "He was on one of his own trains and was killed when another of his own trains ran

Club president Lloyd Aspinwall may not have missed the club's opening after all.
COURTESY OF THE LIBRARY OF CONGRESS

Samuel Spenser still reads his paper in The Annex.
COURTESY OF THE JEKYLL ISLAND MUSEUM ARCHIVES

into him. I think that is the most extraordinary thing," Andersson says.

Spenser may have thought so, too. Folks here suspect he left the fatal accident and returned to the Jekyll Island apartment he loved so well. "I was right there when guests at different times—six months apart or better—came down to report the same story, essentially. They wanted to know who was disturbing their newspaper and coffee." Guests often report that their *Wall Street Journal* has been rearranged and left on the bed. "Of course, our housekeeping people certainly don't go in and rearrange newspapers," Andersson says.

Guests' reports inspired the staff to do some research. "Then we learned that Spenser was a man of some habit," Andersson says. He insisted on having the *Wall Street Journal* delivered to his room every morning. He wanted it folded a certain way and delivered with his coffee. "And each morning, it was his habit to read the paper and drink his coffee."

Apparently, that's his habit still.

While Spenser appears to be spending an extended vacation

Guests often report that their newspaper has been rearranged and their coffee sipped in Samuel Spenser's old room.
COURTESY OF JEKYLL ISLAND CLUB HOTEL

here, a third spirit at Jekyll Island Club gives the term *workaholic* new life. A ghostly bellman still frets over guests' laundry, says a former employee I'll call Fred.

Fred himself worked as a bellman back when people could reach the island only by boat. His job included ferrying guests' laundry to and from a dry cleaner on the mainland. It went like clockwork—unless groomsmen occupied the hotel's second floor.

"On several different occasions, [Fred] talked about going to the second floor to return dry cleaning . . . to men in the wedding party," Andersson says. "He would go to the [groomsmen's] room, knock on the door, not get a response, and go on down the hall." When he finished his rounds, he circled back to knock again. Invariably, when the groomsmen answered and Fred turned to pick up their laundry, it had vanished. Just as invariably, according to Andersson, "the [groomsman] would say, 'It's here. I've already got it.' "

Who delivered it? "On a couple of occasions, as [Fred] was entering that hallway, he saw just a glimpse of a person dressed in those really old-fashioned-looking bellman clothes—the pillbox and striped pants. And our bellmen didn't wear anything like that in [Fred's] day," she says.

Jekyll Island Club is no longer an exclusive private playground, although it still welcomes guests. The state of Georgia now owns the island, its clubhouse, and its cottages, many of which have been restored. (Several cottages have their own ghost stories. The tour guides can clue you in.)

Today's guests enjoy many things the old-time members did, among them golf, tennis, croquet, boating, and outstanding cuisine. When you visit, ask to stay in Samuel Spenser's old suite in The Annex, or on the second floor of the main hotel. The club doesn't publicize its spirits, but the concierge and the tour guides will gladly answer your questions. After a few days, you'll understand why the hotel's trio of spirits is in no hurry to depart.

ADAIRSVILLE

Barnsley Inn and Golf at Barnsley Gardens

597 BARNSLEY GARDENS ROAD
ADAIRSVILLE, GA 30103
770-773-7480
www.barnsleyinn.com
$$$-$$$$

Donna Martin, the garden tour manager at Barnsley Gardens, has seen Godfrey Barnsley's ghost only once, but she's not likely to forget it.

"It was just a dreary, wintry day," she says. "It was November of '95." The resort's formal gardens lay still and bleak with not a tourist in sight, thanks to the weather. One employee was working in the museum—the ruins of the old manor house built by cotton magnate Godfrey Barnsley in the 1800s.

"One of the other gardeners and myself walked up into the gardens," Martin says. "We were getting ready to move some of the

The ruins of the old manor house built by cotton magnate Godfrey Barnsley in the 1800s
COURTESY OF BARNSLEY INN AND GOLF AT BARNSLEY GARDENS

original boxwoods, to place them in the front of the boxwoods parterre."

As they talked, Martin scanned the gardens Godfrey and his wife had planned more than a century earlier. "I looked toward the ruins. There was this image of a man in a black long-tailed coat. He came from the vault—from Godfrey Barnsley's vault—and walked through the woods and down into the ruins."

Her fellow gardener glanced at Martin's face and knew something was wrong. "She said, 'What did you see?' " Martin says.

Reluctantly, Martin told her. Thinking it may have been a visitor she saw, the gardeners searched the grounds. "We went into the ruins, and we walked around into every room. There are no doors or windows. You can see around everywhere. The only person around was [employee] George Adams, who was there so if anybody showed up, he could talk to them." She asked Adams if anyone had entered the manor house. "He said, 'No. I've been up here all day and haven't seen a soul.' I said, 'Ooo-kay.' "

Martin's wasn't the first unusual sighting in the gardens. Guests have often reported seeing Godfrey's wife, Julia.

Godfrey and Julia began their home here in the 1840s. Some say the family was cursed for building a house on a place holy to the Cherokees. Julia and her infant son died of tuberculosis in 1845,

Godfrey Barnsley
One employee saw the image of a man in a black long-tailed coat come from Godfrey Barnsley's vault and walk through the woods, down into the ruins.
COURTESY OF CLENT COKER, BARNSLEY HISTORIAN

Julia Barnsley
Guests have reported seeing Godfrey's wife, Julia, in the gardens.
COURTESY OF CLENT COKER, BARNSLEY HISTORIAN

leaving Godfrey grief-stricken. Soon Godfrey, who communicated with Julia through séances, began seeing her in the gardens and speaking with her.

Even though that information doesn't generally make the garden tour, visitors often ask if there's a ghost in the gardens. "We've had people out here who say they've seen them," Martin says, adding that visitors often see Julia by the fountain.

Godfrey and Julia aren't alone. Witnesses have reported seeing a murdered member of this family on the grounds. Others have seen a Confederate soldier—possibly Colonel Robert G. Earle, who was shot here by Federal soldiers.

As for Martin, who witnessed Godfrey exiting his vault that November day, she's seen nothing unusual since. "I've been here for a little over seven years now, and that was my first little incident. I've walked these gardens at night when it's pitch black, and that was the only time I've ever seen something."

The experience inspired her to do some research. She learned that several people have seen Godfrey exit his vault. Their experience helped validate her own. "I said, 'Well, maybe that *was* him,' " Martin reports.

Today, Godfrey and Julia's old property is home to an eighteen-hole golf course, a spa, tennis courts, a pool, nature trails, guest cottages, and two restaurants. Their manor house, now known simply as "the Ruins," operates as a museum. Barnsley Inn and Golf at Barnsley Gardens is open year-round. Golf and spa packages are available.

If you'd like to meet Julia or Godfrey, try the garden tour.

GRANTVILLE

Bonnie Castle

2 POST STREET
GRANTVILLE, GA 30220
800-261-3090 OR 770-583-3090
www.communitynow.com/bonniecastle
$

Bonnie Castle's ghosts introduced themselves in 1992, a few days after Darwin and Patti Palmer moved into the house. "It was probably eleven or twelve o'clock at night, and we heard this glass crash," Darwin says. He considered investigating. "And I said, 'No, it will still be broken in the morning.' "

Well, maybe not.

"The next day, I was walking around upstairs, downstairs, in the basement, the attic. I didn't find anything at all. So that's when I first started to be impressed. I thought that was quite strange."

Darwin believes two spirits share his home: those of Itura Colley and her daughter-in-law, Mary.

Itura and her husband, J. W., built this house in 1896. Strange, though not supernatural, things started happening almost at once.

Itura, an artist, created mannequins for museums all over the world. "She'd put them around different places to scare people," Darwin says. She enjoyed inviting ministers to stay at her home—and slipping a mannequin into the guest-room bed. The mannequin was a dead ringer for a corpse. "She'd just be laughing," Darwin says affectionately.

Itura had other unsettling notions: "[She] had electricity put in very early, some of it probably when the house was built. And this was probably the first house in town that had running water." Her mannequins are long gone, but Itura still gets antsy when folks mess with the utilities. She slips up behind workers to examine their work and occasionally editorializes by hurling small objects across the room. Once, as a handyman rewired a chandelier, "this Hummel [figurine] flew off the shelf and landed in the middle of the floor and broke into pieces," Darwin says. "Anytime we went to change things that were done in the past years, [the spirits] were reluctant to see the change made."

The spirit of Mary, Itura's daughter-in-law, sometimes manifests

One of Itura's mannequins is scaring her son, Allen, and daughter, Henrietta, in a photograph made circa 1930.
Courtesy of Bonnie Castle

J. W. Colley and his wife, Itura, built Bonnie Castle in 1896.
COURTESY OF BONNIE CASTLE

as an odd, musty odor, Darwin says. He believes Mary also effects the electricity. Once, two visitors dropped in when the house was for sale and the electricity had been disconnected. "They were . . . on the second floor, and [one of the visitors] said they heard this air conditioner kick on downstairs, in the bedroom where the owner stayed." They ran down to Mary's room. "As soon as they got [inside], it kicked off. [The visitor] checked, and the electricity had been turned off to the house."

A three-year-old named Tess met a third spirit here. As she sat on the porch with her mom, she began waving to an unseen person at the gate, inviting him to play. She told her puzzled mother she was talking to a man wearing a yellow shirt, "straps," and a hat. "We thought she was playing games," Darwin says. But then the innkeepers found a photo of Itura's son. In the photograph, he wears a light shirt, suspenders, and a garden hat.

If that *is* her son's spirit at the gate, he has a beautiful place to come home to. This restored twenty-room mansion—complete with turrets, stained glass, and a unique grand staircase—has five guest rooms furnished with antiques, Georgia pottery, and art. Rates include a full breakfast and evening refreshments.

Bonnie Castle, whose guests have included Franklin D. Roosevelt, Jimmy Carter, and Madame Chiang Kai-shek, is listed on the National Register of Historic Places. You'll probably want to focus on the second floor, where guests have reported feeling abrupt changes in temperature and sensing a presence near the prayer bench. "There are certain people who know something's going on, [and] it doesn't take them long to start asking questions," Darwin says. "We don't tell them, of course, unless they express some interest."

Jekyll Island

Jekyll Island Club Hotel. Please see the feature on page 91.

Macon

The 1842 Inn

353 College Street
Macon, GA 31201
800-336-1842 or 912-741-1842
$$-$$$

Joanne Dillard, who handles the front desk at The 1842 Inn, has never seen a ghost, but she says she doesn't doubt the reports placing spirits in this historic inn.

A young female guest who generally liked to stay in the main house experienced the most dramatic encounter. "This particular night, the only room we had available was the Dogwood Room," Dillard says. "She said she felt a little uneasy because of the door opening to the outside." She took the room anyway.

"She stepped out of the shower, dried her body off, and tied the towel around her hair," Dillard says. When she turned to look

John Gresham, the original owner, sits astride a horse in front of what is now The 1842 Inn.
COURTESY OF THE 1842 INN

Guests have also reported experiences with a little girl's spirit at this inn.
COURTESY OF THE 1842 INN

into her bedroom, a man was sitting there, watching her. "The uniform that he was wearing, it had a long, dark jacket. He smiled and bowed his head, and she said his expression told her, 'Don't be afraid. I am here to protect you.' " The apparition never moved, but the guest felt the energy change around her throat. "It just seemed like, right around her neck, there was a warm feeling," Dillard says. "No fingers actually touched her, but she had a warm sensation, a warm, relaxed feeling."

When the guest reported the experience and described the uniform, staff members supplied a portrait of the house's original owner, John Gresham. "There is a picture here of Gresham, and he is wearing that kind of uniform. She said it could have been a younger Mr. Gresham."

Another night, guests in two separate rooms reported an experience with a little girl's spirit.

The first guest saw the child in his room. He said the little girl "stepped through the fireplace," according to Dillard. "The fireplace lit up. She entered the flames, and when she went through, the flames went out."

The second incident took place in the John Gresham Room. The morning afterward, a guest approached Dillard. "He said, 'Last night, a little girl kept pulling on my fingers,' " Dillard says. Each time the guest tried to awaken his wife, the child spirit disappeared. "He stayed the second night, and there was no girl to appear."

Employees have spotted a third spirit in the parlor, in a bedroom, and in the guesthouse. "[One employee] couldn't identify her, but she said she was tall, thin, and blond. Another employee saw the same image," Dillard says.

This Greek Revival inn, which is listed on the National Register of Historic Places, has twenty-one guest rooms, plus sitting rooms, a library, and a courtyard. Rates include a full breakfast served in your room and hors d'oeuvres.

Be sure to request the John Gresham Room or the Dogwood Room.

Don't be afraid to ask about spirits here. The people of Savannah don't mind talking about their ghosts; in fact, they enjoy showing them off. Many of Savannah's house museums, inns, and restaurants are rumored to be haunted. (The best haunted restaurant? The Pirate's House.)

As you might expect, Savannah hosts several ghost tours. Try Savannah by Foot Walking Tours. Owner Greg Profitt offers a "Haunted Tour" and a "Haunted Pubs Tour." For more information, consult www.savannahtours.com.

Hamilton-Turner House

330 HAMILTON ABERCORN STREET
SAVANNAH, GA 31401
888-448-8849 OR 912-233-4800
www.hamilton-turnerinn.com
$$-$$$

The current owners of this inn don't believe in ghosts, says night manager Nancy Hillis. But Hillis does. She's met them.

Hillis owned the house from 1991 to 1997. During that time, her living quarters occupied one section of the ten-thousand-square-foot inn. "The other four apartments, I turned into a bed-and-breakfast," she says.

During restoration, begun in 1991, Hillis began hearing strange sounds. "I kept hearing something over my head that . . . sounded like giggling children, and there were no children up there." Hillis shrugged it off. "I attributed the sound to either a television or [the tenant's] dog. But I kept hearing, and kept *hearing*."

The sounds were always the same. "So I thought, 'Well, it's not a television,'" she says. The dog theory bit the dust the day she left an apartment full of noise, only to find the tenant and her dog sitting outside. Hillis asked the tenant if she ever heard odd sounds in the apartment. "She said, 'You mean like children giggling and pool balls breaking?' She said, 'I hear it all the time.'" Hillis hadn't

The Hamilton-Turner Inn, home to Samuel P. Hamilton who was a Confederate major general and mayor of Savannah, was noted for its lavish parties and the dignitaries who attended them.
COURTESY OF THE HAMILTON-TURNER INN

heard a pool rack breaking, but she tucked the information away, glad to know someone else heard the children.

"In the meantime, I am trying to create a historical museum tour house, so I'm doing a lot of research on the family [who lived here]," she says. "I knew they had five children—four boys and one girl. I also knew that when the house was built in 1873, the top floor was the children's quarters. When I had time, I'd go to the history museum and look through the newspaper clippings."

There were plenty to look through. Samuel P. Hamilton, a major general in the Confederate army, served as mayor of Savannah. His home was noted for its lavish parties and the dignitaries who attended them. "It was always an active house," Hillis says.

One day, she came across a clipping from the late 1890s. "And the newspaper clipping said, 'Last night, the Hamiltons were throwing yet another ball . . . and the Hamilton children misbehaved

The five Hamilton children may be the source for the sounds of children giggling and pool balls breaking in the inn.
COURTESY OF THE HAMILTON-TURNER INN

quite badly.' As a matter of fact, they felt they were missing the party downstairs, and they proceeded to take billiard balls from their billiard table and thrust them down the staircase." The tykes beaned a dignitary, who required several stitches.

That explained the giggles and the billiard balls.

Hillis has never heard the balls clatter down the stairs, but one of her tour guides has. "She took off running and wouldn't come back," she says.

Hillis continued hearing the giggles the seven years she lived in the house. Others, including a skeptical friend, heard the children, too. "It was about 6 P.M. He comes down [from the fourth floor] white as a ghost," Hillis recalls. "He said, 'Who's in the house besides us?' " She told them they were alone. "He said, 'Well, *somebody's* here.' He said, 'I heard giggles. And then I heard somebody say, "Daddy, Daddy-Daddy-Daddy." ' He said it was real clear. Then he heard kind of a swishing noise."

The children's father has also been spotted in the house. "Tour guides have seen him—a milky cast in the form of a man," Hillis says. One visitor reported seeing him at the top of the stairs. "People who came on tours would feel things and see things. They'd write me. Two or three told me they felt the presence of someone having a heart attack—which is what Mr. Hamilton died of."

Hillis believes she once heard Mr. Hamilton on the stairs. "In the middle of the night, I heard a very heavy person running up this stairway. I ran out to the hallway." She looked up the stairs and saw her frightened tenant looking down. "[The tenant] said, 'I've already called the police.' The police went through every room. No one was here, and every outside door was locked."

Visitors often ask if the inn is haunted. "Last night, people . . . staying near the children's quarters saw something milky white go past their window." One of those guests told Hillis a child pushed her arm and cried, "Mom, Mom, Mom."

"I've heard that [from guests] a couple of times," Hillis says.

The child spirits have recently started locking their doors from the inside, she adds. "[Workers have] had to go in and practically take it off of the hinges."

If you want to meet these spirits, ask for rooms on the top floor. If you want to discuss the spirits with Nancy Hillis, you'll find her at the desk most evenings. She won't mention the ghosts—you'll need to ask.

The Kehoe House

123 Habersham Street
Savannah, GA 31401
800-820-1020 or 912-232-1020
$$-$$$

Some guests say Mrs. Kehoe still visits the Renaissance Revival–style home she and her husband, William, built in 1892. "We have had some guests that have said they had strange things happen," says concierge/manager David Harrington.

Ask for room 203 if you visit. "We had a guest who swore that someone was sitting on the edge of her bed at night," Harrington says. Another night, a guest in room 203 saw a ghostly woman writing at the desk.

Some guests say Mrs. William Kehoe still visits the home she and her husband built in 1892.
COURTESY OF THE KEHOE HOUSE

Mrs. Kehoe may also venture upstairs at night to tuck her nine children in. "One of the [former] owners would never sit on the third floor, because he felt someone kiss him on the cheek one night," Harrington adds.

The Kehoe House, renovated in the 1990s, has fifteen guest rooms. Rates include a full breakfast and evening hors d'oeuvres.

Miss Anna Powers, who built 17Hundred90 Inn, still putters about the inn.
COURTESY OF 17HUNDRED90 INN, RESTAURANT, AND LOUNGE

17Hundred90 Inn, Restaurant, and Lounge

307 EAST PRESIDENT STREET
SAVANNAH, GA 31401
800-487-1790 OR 912-236-7122
www.bbonline.com/ga/1790/index.html
$$

This inn was built in 1790 for Miss Anna Powers, who still dwells here.

According to night manager Glenn M. Hofsiss, Anna's lover spent much of his time sailing between Savannah and England, a common route in the 1700s and 1800s, when Georgia cotton fed English mills. One day, her beloved sailed out and never returned. "It's said . . . that Anna, brokenhearted, leapt to her death from the second story of this building," Hofsiss writes.

Anna's spirit still putters about the inn. "Guests have mentioned returning to their rooms and finding their clothes laid out for them in a very meticulous manner," Hofsiss adds. "The last occurrence [was] just a few months ago by a regular guest, who was not so pleased to find her clothes laid out for her [and] was extremely frightened."

Anna's spirit doesn't lack company. According to inn lore, a servant who once lived in the kitchen area scares waitresses by pushing knives and spoons from the table.

Finally, the spirit of a merchant marine ambles about the house. "His image has been seen walking through the wall in our garden room," Hofsiss notes. "Our ghosts are said to be friendly spirits and content with this dwelling, and we welcome them."

The 17Hundred90 Inn has fourteen guest rooms, some with fireplaces. Rates include a continental breakfast and complimentary wine.

The Riverview was built in 1916 as a hotel.
COURTESY OF THE RIVERVIEW HOTEL

ST. MARYS

The Riverview Hotel

105 OSBORNE STREET
ST. MARYS, GA 31558
912-882-3242
www.stmaryswelcome.com
$

"The Riverview was built in 1916 as a hotel," says innkeeper Jerry Brandon, whose family bought the place in the 1920s. The guest in room 8 seems to have missed his checkout time by several decades.

Brandon's ten-year-old sister met that guest in the late 1950s,

The guest in Room 8 of The Riverview Hotel seems to have missed his checkout time by several decades.
COURTESY OF THE RIVERVIEW HOTEL

when the hotel was temporarily closed and the upstairs rooms sat abandoned. "My sister, who is not prone to believing in supernatural-type things, was playing upstairs with one of her friends," he says. "They turned around and saw an apparition that kind of was floating along in the hall, and turned around and looked at them. . . . She swears to this day that could not have been anything but a ghost."

They weren't the first to have an unusual experience here. "In the mid-fifties, there was a gentleman staying here," Brandon says. That gentleman "complained on several occasions that somebody was waking him up in the middle of the night, somebody was sneaking in there and tugging on his leg and running." Another visitor who didn't know the story reported the same experience. Both visitors occupied room 8.

During a regional power outage, the light in the hallway outside room 8 remained lit, he says, adding that this was the very spot where his sister saw the spirit. "Everything down here was out, but we had one light upstairs that was on," he says. "We never could figure out what that was."

Rates here include an expanded continental breakfast. The Riverview Hotel has sixteen guest rooms, a saloon, and a restaurant. The hotel faces the Cumberland Island Ferry; most guests visit the national seashore there.

When you visit, ask for room 8.

SOUTH CAROLINA

Charleston loves its ghost stories, and Georgetown claims to be the Palmetto State's most haunted town. Surprisingly, then, your best chance of meeting a ghost in South Carolina lies inland, in the town of Union. At the Inn at Merridun, the spirits are both friendly and plentiful.

The Inn at Merridun

100 Merridun Place
Union, SC 29379
864-427-7052
www.merridun.com
$-$$

Perfume, Pennies, and Pipe Smoke

What's the surest way to meet a ghost at the Inn at Merridun? Just show up, says innkeeper Peg Waller. "People will say, 'I want to stay in the room where the ghost is.' Actually, that's every room. There are things that go on here that I have no explanation for."

Jim and Peg Waller, who lived in San Diego before moving to Union, bought this house after Jim saw it in an ad. "My husband had a déjà vu feeling," Peg says. Jim flew out to see the house and felt like he was coming home.

The Wallers suspected something was up during renovations, in 1990, when they started finding pennies in the house. "We'd go in and clean a room, and we'd go back and find one in the middle of the floor or on the bed," Peg says.

They were puzzled until they heard an old saying: "It was, 'Pen-

The owners of The Inn at Merridun started finding pennies in the house during renovations.
COURTESY OF THE INN AT MERRIDUN

nies on the floor means money in the door,' " she says. Now, they believe late residents T. C. and Fannie Duncan, who often visit, left the pennies as a housewarming gift. "The smell of an old perfume and the smell of cigar smoke are chronically in the house," Peg says. That's how they know the Duncans have come calling. One guest, an expert on perfumes, recognized the scent as a rose-based formula popular in the nineteenth century.

T. C. and Fannie aren't the only spirits here. According to a clairvoyant who investigated, ten ghosts inhabit the 1855 inn.

A young woman's spirit may be the most distinct. "My husband has seen her. My brother has seen her. I have not," Peg says. "Her name is Mary Anne Wallace. She was a spinster sister of one of the owners back in the 1870s. No on has ever seen her face, but they always describe her. She's short, stout, very buxom. She had on a blue-gray dress. It's a very nubby, linen-ish type of fabric." Peg's husband and brother met the spirit long before the clairvoyant visited, yet the clairvoyant "described the ghost down to the fabric of the dress," Peg says.

"We also have a little white dog in the house." The dog jumps into bed with some guests and growls at others. Peg became aware

The smell of an old perfume and cigar smoke mean Fannie (right) and Thomas Cary Duncan (left) have come calling.
COURTESY OF THE INN AT MERRIDUN

of it when she kept feeling an animal jump on her bed. She first thought it was her cat. "I would turn the light on, and there would be no cat in the room," she says. Jim didn't believe her until one morning when he asked why the cat had spent the night snoozing between them. "The cat hadn't been there all night," Peg laughs.

Music lovers will appreciate another of the inn's ghosts. "We've had guests who woke up to hear harpsichord music," Peg says. "[One couple] heard it, and they listened to it for about forty-five minutes." Another guest reported being serenaded with piano music. The Wallers don't own a harpsichord or a piano.

Another spirit, dubbed "the Red-Headed Ghost," has a fondness for Jim Waller. "Jim, in the middle of the night, will hear someone call his name, . . . or he feels like someone is touching him," Peg says.

The redhead isn't the only spirit who likes to cozy up to folks. One woman reported that a ghost slipped into bed with her and cuddled up "spoon-style." She thought it was her husband. "And when she reached back to touch him, he wasn't there," Peg says. "We have had a couple of women say someone touched them." Another woman reported a man "touching her legs and lying on top of her."

A less sensuous ghost fawns over household appliances. He (or she) first became infatuated with the digital ovens, sometimes locking food inside while it was baking. Until they figured it out, the innkeepers accused each other of sabotaging meals. "We almost got into fistfights about it," Peg laughs. The Wallers' gourmet feasts are now safe, since the spirit has a new interest: the computer. It's often heard fiddling with the keyboard and shuffling papers in the office.

Less-seen spirits at the Inn at Merridun include two young children and an African-American woman. Two Native American spirits who predate the house have been heard playing drums outside.

The inn has five guest rooms and a tearoom. Special packages are available.

Houses along Charleston's Battery
COURTESY OF THE BATTERY CARRIAGE HOUSE INN

CHARLESTON

Charleston brims with history, romance, war stories—and ghosts. Although only a handful of innkeepers publicly claim ghosts, many proprietors and their employees privately admit to interesting goings-on in Charleston's historic inns. If you stay in inns other than those listed here and they feel a little eerie, ask around.

While you're in the city, you might want to try one of Charleston's ghost tours. Consider Low Country Ghost Walk (800-729-3420 or 843-577-3800) or Tour Charleston LLC (800-854-1670).

The Battery Carriage House Inn is one of Charleston's best-known haunted inns.
COURTESY OF THE BATTERY CARRIAGE HOUSE INN

The Battery Carriage House Inn

20 SOUTH BATTERY
CHARLESTON, SC 29401
800-775-5575 OR 843-727-3100
www.virtualcities.com/ons/sc/z/scz6501.htm
$-$$$

Built in 1843, this is one of Charleston's best-known haunted inns. Located on the Battery overlooking the waterfront, it's also one of the most elegant places to stay in the city.

No one knows whose spirit haunts the house, but according to general manager Howard Vroon, the ghost known as "the Carriage House Gentleman" impressed one guest so much that she wrote to the inn to describe her experience. She and her sister had settled in for the night, she said, placing one of the inn's antique chairs against the door to make sure no one entered as they slept. She was surprised, then, when a "wispy gray apparition" floated through the closed door and the chair into the room. The ghost was about five-foot-eight and slight. He glided across the room and lay down beside her, slipping his right arm around her shoulders. "I wasn't frightened, because he didn't seem threatening," the guest wrote. Finally, she spoke to her sister. As her sister answered, the ghost abruptly disappeared.

The Battery Carriage House Inn has eleven garden rooms. Rates include continental breakfast served in the your room or in the garden.

Which room should you ask for? "The most well-known encounter is in number 10," says concierge Nathan Ward.

A spirit at Jasmine House once tore an entire newspaper into three- and four-inch pieces, witnesses say.
COURTESY OF JASMINE HOUSE

Jasmine House

64 HASSELL STREET
CHARLESTON, SC 29401
800-845-7639 OR 843-577-5900
www.aesir.com\jasminehouse
$$-$$$

A temperamental spirit has been reported in this inn's Chrysanthemum Room. In fact, a guest recently called general manager Brien Limehouse to report that a ghost had cornered him in his room.

The guest said he awakened to find the apparition of a woman near his bed. "[He said], 'She wasn't speaking to me, but she was acting very erratic,'" Limehouse says. The guest tried to leave, but his attempts made the spirit angry. "He said she tore up his newspaper into about three- or four-inch pieces—the whole paper. He said, 'I wanted to let you know I didn't make this mess.' "

Limehouse, who went to the room to calm his ruffled guest, says the newspaper was indeed shredded, and the guest's mail was tossed about the room. Nothing like that has happened here since.

The Jasmine House, located in the Ansonborough area of historic Charleston, has ten guest rooms. Rates include breakfast and afternoon hors d'oeuvres and wine. A Jacuzzi is located in the private courtyard.

Meeting Street Inn

173 Meeting Street
Charleston, SC 29401
800-842-8022 or 843-723-1882
www.aesir.com\meetingstreet
$-$$

Guests frequently report hearing and seeing spirits in this nineteenth-century inn.

"The one I experienced firsthand was in room 303," says general manager Brien Limehouse, whose family also owns the Jasmine House. "I'd gotten off work about eleven o'clock," he says. "I told the night manager to call me if there were any problems. About five after midnight, he called." A guest had gone up to find his room dead-bolted—from the inside.

Limehouse headed for the inn with a friend in tow. He, the friend, the night manager, and the guest gathered outside the guest's door. "I assumed, incorrectly, that someone else had gained entry to the room and was in there," Limehouse explains. "I did not suspect a ghost, but [rather] another person, to be in there. So I beat on the door."

When no one answered, he tried his master key. When it wouldn't work on the deadbolt, he headed downstairs for the deadbolt master key. "I had three people standing outside the door while I went down. I go back up there and I say, 'Okay, I think someone's in here, but let's find out.' I unlock the deadbolt. I turn the door handle, and as I push on the door, there is a lot of resis-

The ghost who lives at Meeting Street Inn may have been connected with one of the inn's builders.
COURTESY OF MEETING STREET INN

tance. It feels like someone about 250 pounds or more is pushing. The door actually opens about a quarter-inch and then pushes me back. The power was incredible. Something shut the door like I wasn't even there. I had my foot in it, and it shoved me out. They all saw it," he says, referring to his associates.

By then, Limehouse was shaken. Not only was someone in the room, someone *large* was in the room. He decided to break the door in. "I go, 'One, two, three,' and when we hit the door, it flies open with no resistance whatsoever. So I say, 'Okay, he must be in the closet. . . . He must be under the bed.' "

Finally, they tried the bathroom. Limehouse whispered to his friend, "He must be in the shower." But when he yanked the curtain back, the shower stood empty.

Limehouse turned to his guest. "I said, 'All right, I don't know what's in here. I can't explain what's going on.' " He offered the guest a different room, but the guest declined. "It didn't really scare the guest, but it did me," he says.

Another night, guests in room 107 called the desk and announced that a ghost had just materialized in their room. "They said, 'She just walked out,' " Limehouse says. "I walked down there, and the door was open. They were both sitting in bed."

The stunned couple claimed that a woman had materialized at the foot of their bed. The upper half of her body looked solid, but the bottom half faded away to nothingness. "She floated over, opened the door, and left it open," Limehouse says.

He believes this spirit may have been a family member of one of the inn's builders, who had their living quarters upstairs. He also notes that lights in the inn often go on and off by themselves and that other "little things" occur. "It happens mostly in the back rooms, in an older section [of the inn]," Limehouse says.

The inn's fifty-six guest rooms open to piazzas overlooking a garden courtyard. Rates include continental breakfast, a newspaper, and afternoon refreshments. For your best chance of encountering a spirit, request room 303 or room 107.

Georgetown

DuPre House Bed-and-Breakfast

921 Prince Street
Georgetown, SC 29440
877-519-9499 or 843-546-0298
www.duprehouse.com
$-$$

Innkeepers Richard and Judy Barnett don't think they have any nonpaying guests. But they've had several odd experiences since buying this inn in March 2000. And former owners and employees tell a slew of ghost stories about this 1740 inn. In fact, a child's spirit has long been associated with the house.

According to a former innkeeper, the child spirit made her first appearance during a renovation, when a passerby reported her climbing out of a third-story window. Months later, the innkeeper heard a child on the second floor calling for her mother. In both cases, no actual children were present.

Guests also describe unusual experiences upstairs. One man reported seeing puffs of smoke in a second-floor bathroom and seeing a child materialize in the smoke. Another guest smelled smoke in the house when there was no fire and glimpsed a woman in a long dress and an apron.

Former employees claim items upstairs have a habit of rearranging themselves. Most interestingly, a former innkeeper and a guest saw a child's footprints on a newly vacuumed carpet in a third-floor bedroom. The tiny footprints led from the door to a blank wall but didn't return.

All of this activity may relate to a widow and her child who lived here just after the Civil War. When the house caught on fire, the widow got her child out but died in the blaze herself.

Is there any truth to the ghost stories?

The Barnetts remain skeptical but admit that unusual things have happened in the seven months they've owned the house. "Last week, we had two ladies here [who] said somebody was coughing in the bedroom above them, and they also heard water running on the third floor and little footprints going up and down the stairs," Judy says.

Another guest reported hearing a child playing on the third

A child's spirit has long been associated with the DuPre House Bed-and-Breakfast.
COURTESY OF DUPRE HOUSE BED-AND-BREAKFAST

floor. "She thought she heard the little girl humming a child's tune," Richard says. "The story was that she sounded like a happy little girl, playing and so forth."

And several people have seen a smoky mist with no obvious source. "A friend of ours was here, and she and her husband were helping paint," Richard says. "And she was taking a break, sitting out back. . . . And about ten or fifteen yards away from her, the ground appeared to be smoking. It looked like steam—it was sort of smoky-looking. It was just that spot."

Richard didn't see the mist. "But at least four or five other people did, including my wife," he says. "It was after that that we heard the ghost story. The old cookhouse had been at that spot. The fire the woman was involved in . . . involved the cookhouse."

DuPre House Bed-and-Breakfast has five guest rooms furnished with antiques and reproductions. Its verandas overlook the gardens and pool. Rates include a full breakfast and afternoon and evening refreshments.

Be sure to ask for an upstairs room.

1790 House Bed-and-Breakfast

630 Highmarket Street
Georgetown, SC 29440
800-890-7432 or 843-546-4821
www.1790house.com
$-$$

A female spirit in this eighteenth-century West Indies–style plantation house has snuggled up to at least one guest, says innkeeper John Wiley. But she may not be the spirit who welcomed Wiley soon after he and his wife, Patricia, opened this bed-and-breakfast.

"Shortly after we moved into the inn, I was here in the house one night by myself," John recalls. "I guess it was probably about 11:15 p.m., and I was in the laundry room folding the last load of towels." The laundry room is located on the ground level; the main floor occupies the second level.

A female spirit has snuggled up to at least one guest at the 1790 House Bed-and-Breakfast.
COURTESY OF 1790 HOUSE BED-AND-BREAKFAST

Much of the inn's activity takes place in or near the Rice Planter's Room.
COURTESY OF 1790 HOUSE BED-AND-BREAKFAST

"I was downstairs, and I heard about four or five heavy footsteps stomping across right above my head. It startled me. . . . I ran upstairs and looked around. I checked the doors. Everything was locked and still secure. I, to this day, do not know what those footsteps were. It definitely was four or five heavy footsteps, walking."

John shrugged the incident off, but before long, others started reporting unusual experiences—usually in the vicinity of the Rice Planter's Room, where the closet doors swing open at odd times. One guest met a spirit there. "During the night, he felt the presence of a woman put her arm around his shoulders," John says. "It startled him, and he woke up and could feel the presence. He could see a woman in a filmy gown, and he turned over, and it disappeared."

The nine-year-old granddaughter of an employee may have spoken with the same spirit. The employee heard the girl chatting with someone. "The granddaughter came out and asked her if she saw the lady she was talking to," John says. "She said she was in a white, filmy dress. She said she was a real nice lady."

Odd things also happen on the third floor, in the room over the Rice Planter's Room. "We've had stories of the bed shaking for no apparent reason," John says. Closet doors open on their own here and in nearby rooms.

The room just beneath the Rice Planter's Room also sees its share of activity. "We had one of our guests [in that room] ask us what kind of spirits we had," John says. "He woke up and could hear his cam recorder playing. He said, 'I turned that off. About an hour later, it came on again.' He was wondering what was going on."

Who is this restless spirit?

"The only tale of a spirit in the house is there was a small child who died in his mother's arms in one of the bedrooms. The story is if you put a rocking chair in [the Rice Planter's Room], it will rock in the night."

The Wileys don't keep a rocking chair in that room, but a young guest asked for one, to test the story. "He said about an hour after they went to bed, it started to rock." John hasn't tested the story, but visitors are welcome to, he says.

This bed-and-breakfast is located in Georgetown's National Historic District. It features a wraparound veranda, gardens, and six guest rooms with private baths and sitting areas. Rates include a full breakfast and evening refreshments.

Ask for the Rice Planter's Room.

Moncks Corner

In the Heron Room of Rice Hope Plantation, it has been reported through the years that a rocking chair rocks at night.
COURTESY OF RICE HOPE PLANTATION

Rice Hope Plantation

206 RICE HOPE DRIVE
MONCKS CORNER, SC 29461
800-569-4038 OR 843-761-1866
www.ricehope.com
$

A little girl's spirit has occupied this site for centuries, according to innkeeper Lou Edens.

"This is a true story that happened in the 1700s," says Edens. "At that time, Rice Hope Plantation was known as Luckins Plantation. The [little girl's] grandfather owned the plantation."

Rice Hope, the seat of Dr. William Read, taken from one of the Rice Fields
C. 1796 WATERCOLOR ON PAPER BY CHARLES FRASER
COURTESY OF GIBBES MUSEUM OF ART / CAA, 1938.036.0093

When the child's father died, her mother remarried and sent the girl to a nearby boarding school run by a man named Gutar. "He was very strict," Edens says. One day, the little girl misbehaved. "The schoolmaster tied her to a tombstone at Strawberry Chapel as punishment—and forgot about her." She struggled against the ropes as darkness fell.

"A slave had been out wandering . . . that night," Edens says. "He was returning, and he heard the child whimper. He went in the graveyard and found the child tied to the tombstone. And so he spread the alarm. They released the child, and she was unharmed—other than emotionally scarred." Rescuers took her to the plantation and her grandmother's comforting arms.

The schoolmaster didn't fare as well. "There was a furor against him," Edens says with satisfaction. The villagers placed his family on a ferry and sent them on their way. "Then they tied the schoolmaster on the back of a mule backwards and slapped the mule. The mule left, and the schoolmaster was never heard from again."

As for the little girl, her grandmother still comforts her in this old plantation house. "It's in the room that overlooks the river,"

Edens says. "We call it the Heron Room. There's a rocking chair there that rocks at night. This has been reported through the years." Guests in this and adjoining rooms hear objects moving, voices whispering, and doors opening and closing.

Lou Edens has moved the rocking chair out of the Heron Room to make way for a television and to keep from frightening her guests, but she'll gladly replace it for curious visitors.

The original plantation burned, and Rice Hope was rebuilt in 1840 on its foundations. The house, renovated in 1929 by United States senator John S. Frelinghuysen of New Jersey, eventually fell into ruin but was restored and opened as an inn in 1987.

Rice Hope Plantation, with its five guest rooms and a two-hundred-year-old formal garden, overlooks the Cooper River. Rates include a full breakfast and access to the boat landing and the tennis courts. Canoes are available.

Ask for the Heron Room.

Montmorenci

Annie's Inn Bed-and-Breakfast

3083 Charleston Highway (US 78)
Montmorenci, SC 29829
803-649-6836
www.theinnside-scoop.com/anniesinn.htm
$-$$

The ghost of a little girl calls for her mother in this plantation house, according to owner Scottie Ruark.

"When we first bought the house nineteen years ago, we heard it all the time," says Ruark. "It was just the eeriest thing. It'd say, 'Mama, Mama.' At first when I heard it, I thought, 'My God, the girls are home from college.'

"It's an actual voice. It's scary."

Ruark, who's operated the inn since 1984, says the voice seems to be lost. If Ruark is downstairs, it sounds like the little girl is upstairs. "You'd be upstairs, it would be coming from downstairs,"

A ghost of a little girl calls for her mother in Annie's Inn Bed-and-Breakfast.
COURTESY OF ANNIE'S INN BED-AND-BREAKFAST

she says. "Some of the guests have also told me they have heard a child calling for its mother."

The two-story plantation house, once the heart of a two-thousand-acre cotton plantation, was built around 1830. It originally stood three stories tall. It was taken down a peg during the Civil War, when cannon fire destroyed the upper story. In the late 1800s, the house became a country doctor's home and hospital. Ruark suspects the little girl is connected with the hospital.

"We also kept hearing a huge, old dinner gong, and we heard bagpipes playing," she says, noting that some of the Civil War troops stationed near the house played the bagpipes. "We had a lot of strange things. But it seemed after the renovations, things calmed down."

Guests here like to rock on the wraparound front porch and to gather around the wood-burning cookstove in the kitchen. Rates include a full breakfast. The inn has a pool, private rooms, and guest cottages. Montmorenci is located about five miles from Aiken.

Mount Pleasant

If you want to meet Captain Samuel Guilds's ghost, visit Guilds Inn during a full moon or a storm.
Courtesy of Guilds Inn

Guilds Inn

101 Pitt Street
Mount Pleasant, SC 29464
800-331-0510 or 843-881-0510
www.guildsinn.com
$$

If you want to meet Captain Samuel Guilds's ghost, visit Guilds Inn during a full moon or a storm, advises owner Lou Edens, who is also the proprietor of Rice Hope Plantation. It's during full moons and storms that the old tugboat captain slips up the fire escape and enters the third floor of this 1888 inn.

"We're pretty sure it is Captain Guilds, who was the owner of this house from 1919 until his death in the 1960s," Edens says. "He comes in through the fire escape and leaves the door ajar. People report hearing footsteps in the hall during the night."

Guilds usually visits room 6 when he comes calling. Edens suspects this was a meeting place for Guilds and the lover he met after his wife's death. "He sits on the bed and rearranges the crocheted canopy," she says. "You can see where somebody's been sitting on the bed."

He also visits the second-floor dining room during storms. "He rearranges the chairs," Edens says. "Soon after I bought the inn, we had a hurricane scare. We battened down the hatches and took a lot of precautions. After it had passed, we started opening the house. I noticed that Captain Guilds's portrait had been removed from over the mantelpiece in the dining room. The light was unplugged, and the portrait was sitting on the floor in front of the fireplace." Edens checked with workers. No one had removed the portrait or unplugged its light. "No one in the house had touched it," she says. Except, perhaps, Captain Guilds.

"Guilds seems to be very interested in our international visi-

After a storm, the owner noticed that Captain Guilds's portrait had been removed from over the mantelpiece in the dining room, but no one had removed the portrait.
COURTESY OF GUILDS INN

tors," she adds. "One night, we had an ambassador staying here, and when he left, the picture over the bed was turned diagonally."

He particularly reacts to German visitors and has zeroed in on a frequent guest named Dusty. "Captain Guilds harasses Dusty," Edens chuckles. "One night, Dusty was staying on the third floor." He awakened to find that "the mirror behind the dresser was removed from the wall and [had] slid down behind the dresser. One night recently, one of the globes [in Dusty's room] just fell off of the sconce." Guilds sometimes sounds an alarm when Dusty checks in. "We occasionally have a false fire alarm with our system. And I don't think it's ever happened except when Dusty was in residence," Edens says.

She admits she didn't believe in ghosts when she acquired the inn in 1996. "I challenged him on the last full eclipse of the millennium," she chuckles. "I figured that if he was gonna come out, he would come for that eclipse. The eclipse was occurring right at midnight."

Edens went into room 6. "I thought, 'Well, I'll just get in this whirlpool tub and wait for him.' " As she settled into the tub, the washcloth jumped off the towel rack and the shower rod crashed down behind her head. "I streaked down two flights of stairs and locked myself in my room," she laughs. "I didn't even come to the inn during the next eclipse."

Guilds *has* brushed against her, she says. "I was in the butler's pantry down the hall from the fire-escape door. It felt like something whisked by and touched my face. It was enough for me to turn around and look behind me. And there was nothing there."

This Colonial Revival structure was built around 1888. It has served Mount Pleasant as a grocery store, a hardware store, a boardinghouse, an office, and a residence. Restored in 1985, the inn has six guest rooms furnished with period reproductions. It also offers a café. Rates include a continental breakfast.

Visit during a full moon or a storm, and ask for room 6.

North Augusta

A woman's spirit still tends the twenty-two-room Rosemary Hall.
Courtesy of Rosemary Hall

Rosemary Hall

804 Georgia Avenue
North Augusta, SC 29841
800-531-5578 or 803-278-6222
www.rosemaryhall.com
$-$$

A woman's spirit still tends this twenty-two-room mansion, employees say. Some people see her; others sense her. Night manager Mary Terry does both.

"It's a gift, I think," says Terry, who began working here in 1993. "It happens to me a lot. I see things. I feel cool breezes. I see shadows—especially Mrs. Jackson's."

Mrs. Jackson was the wife of North Augusta's founding father, James U. Jackson, who completed the inn in 1902. Rosemary Hall has a veranda with fifty-foot columns, but it may be best known for the English staircase in its foyer—and for the spirit who dwells here.

The ghost of Mrs. James U. Jackson has been seen on the grand English staircase.
COURTESY OF ROSEMARY HALL

Terry and other employees often catch a glimpse of Mrs. Jackson in the upstairs halls. "I always see a lady with a shawl on," says Terry, who recognizes Mrs. Jackson from her portrait. "She's short. She's just walking through the house. I've seen her in the staircase and upstairs, around room 205."

A few guests have also spotted the apparition. "Elderly people are very difficult to understand," Terry says, referring to Mrs. Jackson. "Sometimes I get the feeling that if people don't treat her house right, she will get upset."

Mrs. Jackson enjoys pranks. "We've had stuff disappear or [get] changed around. We go back, and it's not there. A lot of the people that work here, they get upset, but it doesn't bother me. Another lady here used to see her and feel her also. She'd say she felt this cool breeze. I'm about the only one that works here that's not afraid to be here."

Rosemary Hall was completely renovated and restored in 1992, as was a second house, Lookaway Hall, built by James Jackson's brother, Walter. Both are listed on the National Register of Historic Places and hold Four-Diamond ratings from AAA. The inns have twenty-three guest rooms total. They're decorated with antiques, many original to the homes. Mrs. Jackson prefers Rosemary Hall, and folks interested in ghosts probably will, too.

Ask for room 205.

Before riding down the oak allée, the late Dr. Tucker still rings the bell at the gate centuries later, so his servant will meet him at the carriage house.
COURTESY OF LITCHFIELD PLANTATION

Litchfield Plantation

KINGS RIVER ROAD
P.O. BOX 290
PAWLEYS ISLAND, SC 29585
800-869-1410 OR 843-237-9121
www.litchfieldplantation.com
$$-$$$

Never mind that he's been dead for two centuries. At Litchfield Plantation, the doctor is *in*.

This prosperous rice plantation was founded in 1740. "It was built by one family, but they didn't hold it very long," says Litchfield's front desk manager, Terry Belanger. "A second family took over and held it a little over a hundred years. They were rice planters from Bermuda. The son of the family was a doctor."

Dr. Tucker took his work seriously. "The story goes that he was a well-thought-of, well-liked man" whose practice revolved around his neighbors, both black and white. "He added a one-room wing to the house, which was his office and dispensary and so forth," Belanger says.

"When he would be called out in the middle of the night, he would ride out, and on [his] return, at the gate, at the front of the property, there was a big bell hanging there. He'd ring the bell. By the time he rode down the oak allée, the servant would have come out from the carriage house and would be ready to take his horse." The weary Dr. Tucker would walk from the carriage house to his home. "He would go through his office up the back stairs—which is this tiny, almost vertical stairway—to the second floor, to what we now call the Blue Room, which was his bedroom."

Death hasn't kept Dr. Tucker from his house calls.

"Supposedly, after he passed away, within weeks, people on the plantation and in the neighboring area started hearing the bell ringing at night. It scared them pretty bad," Belanger says. "It rang pretty continually. After a while, they stopped being so scared and started being annoyed. So finally, they took [the bell] down and buried it."

But that didn't stop Dr. Tucker.

"We have had two separate guests, on separate occasions, who have come to check out asking what the bell was that was ringing in the night," she says. "It's claimed that people have seen the doctor walking between the carriage house and the main house.

"And then I have spoken to a guest myself who, when he came in to check out, asked me if anyone had seen the doctor. I said, 'As far as I know since *I've* been here, no.' He said he had. He said he . . . woke in the middle of the night, and the doctor was sitting next to the fireplace. He said he was sitting in a chair, legs crossed, very calmly. And he said he leapt up and turned on his light, and by the time he did that, everything was gone. He was absolutely positive that the doctor was there."

Belanger isn't surprised that the doctor seemed peaceful. "It's a very, very peaceful, calm house. You feel like the people who lived here were good families, living good, fun lives."

The doctor may have visited at least one other guest, she adds.

"We also have one other guest who can be very trying and has visited many times." On one occasion, when this difficult guest happened to be the only visitor in the plantation house, the staff placed him in the Blue Room. The guest "had made pretty much a nuisance of himself," Belanger says.

Apparently, Dr. Tucker took offense.

"This guest called the gate on four different occasions during the night and twice forced the guard to come up to the house and search the house," Belanger says. The guest heard "people climbing the stairs and talking. We decided it was the doctor," she laughs.

Litchfield Plantation is noted for its often-photographed oak allée, which is around four hundred years old. Amenities include an oceanfront clubhouse, a heated pool, the Carriage House Club, a private marina, and two tennis courts.

Request the Blue Room—or another room or suite in the plantation house. Other accommodations are located in a guesthouse and in guest cottages.

SUMMERVILLE

Price House Cottage

224 Sumter Avenue
Summerville, SC 29483
843-871-1877
www.bbonline.com/sc/pricehouse
$$

The ghosts connected with this property reside primarily in the main house, built in 1812, says David Price, who operates the inn with his wife, Jennifer. "The owners from whom we bought the house claimed to have seen a female. Our experiences have been primarily poltergeists and 'funny little things,'" he says.

It didn't take David long to meet his ghost.

"When I first moved into the house in 1974, one of the first nights, about five minutes after I went to bed, I heard water running," he says. David, who was alone in the house, leapt up and

The spirit that lingers in Price House Cottage is playful and likes jewelry.
COURTESY OF PRICE HOUSE COTTAGE

darted toward the noise. "The spigots in the bathroom tub and the sinks were open full," he says. He turned off the water but could find no one else in the house. Puzzled, he returned to bed.

His second clue that something was afoot came via an old grandfather clock. "Finally, we got to the point where we had it running all day long, but it would stop running five minutes after we went to bed at night," David says. It didn't matter what time the couple settled in—eight, ten, twelve. "As soon as we retired, it would go out. After a few weeks, everything settled down, and we didn't have any more problems with it."

Even though the clock hands no longer freeze, the spirit still walks through the house. "The head of our bed backs up to the master bathroom, and every few months we'll be asleep and wake up with a start. You can hear footsteps—very heavy, deliberate footsteps, like someone pacing in the bathroom," David says. "The first thought you have is, 'There's an ax murderer in the house,' and then you realize, 'Well, it's just a ghost again.' We actually go back to sleep."

Jennifer Price believes she bumped into the ghost. "I was going down the center hall one night, and David wasn't home," she says. "That's usually when I hear the ghost, is when David is not here. I physically bumped into something. It was just a soft bump." Jennifer looked around the darkened hall. "As I looked to the right, it just looked like a little bit of light in the living room, a glow." She called out, but no one answered.

The Prices aren't the only ones who have met the spirit. "This has been experienced by a number of people who are skeptical of these things," David says. "We've had numerous people in the house who did not know we had ghosts, who would be aware of something going past them. They don't see anything or feel anything. They see something out of the corner of their eye. They'll see something and turn around and say, 'What was that?' "

One Christmas, the Prices were entertaining friends. "They were sitting so that both of them were facing the center hall," David says. "All of a sudden, their eyes opened real wide, and they both said at the same time, 'Who is that who just walked through the center hall?' Both had seen something, but they couldn't describe what they had seen. The candles had also flickered at the time."

David doesn't know whose spirit lingers in the old house, but it's playful and likes jewelry. "We have all kinds of things that get taken and then appear in the oddest places," he says.

For instance, his daughter's ring once turned up missing, according to David. "About four years later, I was cleaning out a storage area under a bookshelf where I had been throwing old paperback books. I got all the way to the back of this place and picked up my college *Roget's Thesaurus*. I felt it, and it had a lump in it. I opened it up, and here was this ring." The ring's owner took the news in stride. "My daughter, who is now in her early thirties, she would tell us when she was five or six that she was having tea under the house with a ghost. It was a presence that she felt very comfortable with. It was a very real experience."

Another jewelry incident? A few years ago, David lost a silver medallion. "I looked in all the likely places and didn't find it." Since they were remodeling, the Prices moved to the cottage out back. "One night, we went out to dinner, and when we came back in, I opened the back door of the cottage, and dead center on the threshold was this medallion. It had not been there when we left."

David is currently missing a pair of sapphire cuff links. "They haven't turned up, but I know they will. I don't really feel like calling my insurance company and trying to explain how a ghost has taken my jewelry," he laughs.

The Prices operate the eight-hundred-square-foot cottage behind the main house as a bed-and-breakfast. It has a sitting room with a fireplace, a bedroom, a full kitchen, and a bath. They serve a gourmet breakfast in the cottage, on the patio, or (on weekends) in the main house.

"Guests are usually not [in the main house] except at breakfast or in the evening if they come up to have a drink with us," David says. "But certainly, if someone comes who has an interest in the ghost, we'd make every opportunity available for them to fulfill their interest. It's just kind of old hat with us."

If you want to meet this spirit, take David up on his offer to spend time in the main house. And wear interesting jewelry.

The Inn at Merridun. Please see the feature on page 112.

Juxa Plantation

117 Wilson Road
Union SC 29379
864-427-8688
www.bbonline.com/sc/juxa/index.html
$

Nola Bresse owns and operates this bed-and-breakfast, built around 1828. She has never met the woman some people hear singing upstairs and has never seen the ghostly couple guests report finding at the foot of their bed. But she has come face to face with a kindly ghost in the property's cemetery. He made such an impression on her that she talks about him as if they met yesterday.

Bresse was cleaning up the cemetery, getting ready for a historic-homes tour. She was burning some leaves and watching her

The spirit of Jebu Gregory may have come calling at Juxa Plantation.
COURTESY OF JUXA PLANTATION

dogs play. "And suddenly, somebody was looking at me," she says. "I looked up, and there he stood."

To this day, Bresse doesn't know why she didn't scream. The spirit simply didn't inspire fear—not in her, and not in her dogs. "He was tall and thin, and he was gray and white. He had on a jacket longer than today's, and cuffs that were deep and wide, and kind of a mandarin collar. His pant legs were barrel-like, not creased like pants today. He had long arms and a long, wispy, pointed beard—white. He just stood there watching me. I wasn't afraid or anything. The dogs just kept prancing around."

She saw him several times that day. "I would go back to work, and I'd feel someone watching me again, and I would look up."

Later, she described the man to members of the Gregory family, who built the house. "They said, 'Oh yeah, that's a Gregory,'" Bresse laughs, saying they keyed in on the spirit's height and his long arms, which were family traits. (When you visit, check out the staircase, built around 1828, when steps were usually steep and shallow. You'll find exceptionally deep stairs for the time, and a very low railing—for folks with long arms.)

Who is the spirit? Bresse thinks she knows. When she and her family first spruced up the old home, she found two broken headstones in the smokehouse. She pieced them together and placed them in the cemetery. One read, "Jehu Gregory—a Kind and Indulgent Father." And that, she believes, is the spirit she met in the graveyard.

She hasn't seen the tall, gray ghost since, but others have reported strange incidents in the house. "My daughter would hear singing upstairs, and the lights would go on and off," she says. Her son reported standing before a light switch that flipped up and down by itself. "I've had guests say, 'Somebody was tugging on my pillow last night,' " Bresse says. "Another guest heard a man and a woman arguing at the foot of their bed."

If the ghosts are departed Gregorys, perhaps they are comforted to see the Gregory family return for reunions from time to time.

This bed-and-breakfast has three guest rooms. It serves a full breakfast, as well as wine and cheese in the afternoon. Guests are free to explore the gardens, doze in the hammocks, visit the antique shop, fish the five-acre pond, and help feed the horses, goats, and Rhode Island Reds.

They're also free to take the path to the cemetery to pay Jehu Gregory a call.

NORTH CAROLINA

You'll find haunted inns scattered across the Tar Heel State. One of North Carolina's best-known ghosts, the Pink Lady, resides in Asheville.

The Grove Park Inn Resort and Spa

209 Macon Avenue
Asheville, NC 28804
800-438-0050 or 828-252-2711
www.groveparkinn.com
$$-$$$

The Pink Lady

There used to be two rules of conversation for employees of the Grove Park Inn in Asheville: Don't talk about blizzards, and *never* talk about the Pink Lady. Snow spooks people who aren't used to driving mountain roads. And the Pink Lady, an elegant young woman who has haunted this exclusive mountain resort for the better part of a century, spooks people, period.

Until the 1980s, the Grove Park Inn stifled reports of the spirit in room 545—not that she made it easy. The Pink Lady, who's often seen wearing a 1920s-style pink evening gown, locks doors, tickles feet, chats with children, cozies up to law enforcement officers, and drifts down to the inn's nightclub for a little corporeal nightlife.

Is the Pink Lady willing to meet me? Perhaps. Ghost researcher Joshua Warren agrees to introduce us—if the Pink Lady's willing. I check into room 545 and wait.

If you want to stay in room 545, make reservations well in advance. The Pink Lady is most active in cool weather and likes cheerful people, so enter smiling.
COURTESY OF NORTH CAROLINA DIVISION OF TOURISM, FILM AND SPORTS DEVELOPMENT

"I don't claim that I can get rid of ghosts," Warren says, settling into a chair in room 545. "I'm not an exorcist. I claim to be able to come in and say whether or not I find evidence of a ghost. A lot of people wrongly call me a ghost buster. I'm more of a ghost researcher."

Based on instrument findings, photographs, inn lore, and scores of interviews, Warren believes the Pink Lady has haunted this inn since the 1920s, when she tumbled from an interior balcony to the Palm Court two stories below. Who was she in life? Nobody knows. Warren suspects her death was hushed up to protect the inn's reputation and/or the murderer. It's a plausible theory.

In the Roaring Twenties, Asheville was the bee's knees, and the Grove Park Inn was *the* place to be. From presidents to divas, the Jazz Age's elite danced, dined, slumbered, and misbehaved within these massive stone walls. Among many others, the inn welcomed F. Scott Fitzgerald, Henry Ford, Thomas Edison, Harry Houdini, Henri Caruso, and Presidents Wilson and Coolidge.

"The information released to the public was very strictly controlled to maintain an image," says Warren, who notes that the family who owned the inn also owned the local newspaper. To make present-day research even more difficult, the Grove Park Inn didn't archive its guest records from the 1920s, and courthouse fires consumed local death records.

Although the Pink Lady also prowls the sixth floor of the original section of the inn, several psychics have pinpointed room 545 as the Pink Lady's place of death. Warren didn't know that when he began his research in 1995. He and associate Mark-Ellis Bennett met the Pink Lady after a photo revealed a cloud of orange light over room 545's door. Using a magnetometer, they located a pocket of electromagnetic energy by the door connecting the Pink Lady's room and room 547.

Bennett now sits by that connecting door. He places a magnetometer on his chair arm as Warren explains the theory behind their work. "All matter is made up of electrical charge," he says. "There is a 3-D field of energy around all living things." The investigators believe that energy can remain behind after death.

"But couldn't those energy fields radiate from the television?" I ask. "Or wiring in the wall?"

Warren shakes his head. While electronic devices create a fairly constant energy field, the pool that he and Bennett previously measured at the Grove Park Inn fluctuated between 1 and 8 on the magnetometer's scale—its extremes. He believes it was the Pink Lady's energy that they recorded. "It felt like a force, neutral in temperature," he says.

What are the chances the Pink Lady will visit tonight?

Slim, Warren replies. She's most active in cool, crisp weather, and this June night is warm and muggy.

But suddenly the magnetometer's needle jumps, wavers between 1 and 3, dies away, and leaps again. "She's here!" Bennett says.

"Great," I say. "But who is she? Did the psychics give you a name?"

One psychic suggested Ann, Warren says, and a last name beginning with the letter H.

Bennett, who holds the magnetometer, addresses the ghost: "Is your name Ann?" The needle jumps to 8, the highest reading possible. I pass my hand through the pool of energy and the hair on my arm stands up. "Does your last name start with an H?" Bennett asks. The needle goes stone still.

Until the 1980s, the Grove Park Inn stifled reports of the Pink Lady in room 545—but she did not make it easy.
COURTESY OF GROVE PARK INN RESORT AND SPA

If it was the Pink Lady, she's gone.

A few adventure-free minutes later, we take the elevator down to the Palm Court, beneath the Pink Lady's door. "This is where she would have landed if she went over the balcony," says Warren, who believes the Pink Lady died here. He holds out the magnetometer. Again the needle jumps, registering a steady pool of energy.

Later that night, after Warren and Bennett leave, I write a note to the Pink Lady: "I'm here to record any message you would like to send. If you need help, I will try to help you. Please reply." I place the pad on a chair arm.

As I mull over the day's events, the year 1923 pops into my mind. Puzzled, I jot the year on the bottom of the page, as a note to myself—"1923?"—and go to bed.

In the middle of the night, I hear a quiet bell. I look at the clock—1:24. It's the voice-mail bell, but the signal light isn't flashing, and there's no message. I drift back to sleep, not realizing that the bell might later prove to be important.

The next day, I begin interviewing Grove Park Inn employees.

Freda Baker, a bookkeeper, first met the Pink Lady in 1981. The inn had closed to guests for the winter, and Baker was working late. "Time gets away from you," she says. "Seven o'clock came, nine o'clock, eleven o'clock. I realized I was there by myself. I thought, 'Hmm, it's time to leave.' "

Baker hopped in her car, only to find both driveways chained. She tried to reenter the inn but discovered that the door was locked. "I got back in the car and thought, 'I'll sit here with the lights on, and the security guard will see me and open the chain for me,' " she says. "I looked up, and all the lights on the sixth floor of the main inn came on." Thinking that the lone security guard was inside, she honked her horn to get his attention. That's when she saw that the guard was *outside*, walking up the drive. The sixth-floor lights went out and came on again. "It really didn't strike me right then as something being wrong," she says.

Believing someone had entered the building, Baker and the guard took the elevator to the sixth floor. "We got up there, and there wasn't a single light on," she says. "It kind of hit us both at the same time that there was no central light switch. You'd have to flip every light on at the same time." She laughs. "We hightailed it out of there."

Baker has sensed the spirit many times since. "I have not actually seen a Pink Lady," she says. "It's more of a feeling. You'll hear doors open and close, footsteps. You go and look, and there's not a soul there."

But Pat Franklin, who manages a nightclub in the newer section of the inn, not only sees the Pink Lady, she counts her as a regular. In fact, she's had to skirt the pink cloud that sometimes floats around the club. Security personnel are so unnerved by the Pink Lady's comings and goings that they have refused to staff the nightclub—which now sports the Grove Park Inn's only electronic surveillance system.

Still, the Pink Lady is most active in the original section of the inn, which was built in 1913. Guests and employees hear her footsteps and laughter in the halls and bump into her on the stairwell.

Elevator operator Ted Scales swears she rings him to the fifth floor when the main inn is empty. And she awakened the president of the North Carolina Women's Press Association one night by tickling her feet. Security good-naturedly lets locked-out guests back into Room 545 and calls repairmen when she bolts bathroom doors from inside. The hardware has been replaced; she adapts.

The Pink Lady loves children and enters locked rooms to chat with them. They ask about "that nice lady who came and talked to me" or "the lady in the pink dress," says Bill Kelley, the inn's former director of security.

She also likes policemen. Kitty Hawk chief of police Bob Morris, who'd never heard of the Pink Lady when he checked into room 545, met her when she sat down behind him on his bed. When Morris felt the other side of the bed sag, he thought it was a friend playing a prank—until he turned around and found he was alone. He quickly demanded another room.

My second night in the Pink Lady's room, I settle in for a good night's sleep. Again, I am awakened by a bell. Again, I look at the clock: 1:24. Again, it's the voice-mail bell, but there is no light, no message.

Later, I stop by the main desk with some questions. Is someone calling me every night at 1:24 A.M.? Are there glitches in the voice-mail system? Is this happening in other rooms? The clerk checks. No one called or tried to leave a message at 1:24 either night; there are no problems in the line; no one else experienced a problem.

Back in my room, I glance at my note to the Pink Lady: "I'm here to record any message you would like to send. If you need help, I will try to help you. Please reply." Then I glance at what I scribbled at the bottom of the pad: "1923?" Could 1:24 be her answer?

A few hours later, I'm in the public library scrolling through microfilm of the *Asheville Citizen*. The date I'm looking for: 1:24, 1923. January 24, 1923.

On an inside page, I find a drawing of a beautiful young woman who was, the paper says, murdered in a Miami resort hotel. "This can't be part of the Pink Lady's story," I think. Still,

In the Roaring Twenties, the Grove Park Inn was the place to be.
COURTESY OF GROVE PARK INN RESORT AND SPA

I read on. According to the story, Edgar Frady visited his wife, Dorothy, at Miami's "fashionable Flamingo Hotel." They argued, as usual. Her phone rang, and Edgar, believing her lover was calling, shot her. Dorothy fell onto the bed. Edgar then rushed into the bathroom and slit his own throat. Hotel workers, hearing the pistol shots, broke down the locked door. "He killed me," Dorothy said just before she died.

Could the story be a message from the Pink Lady? Both beautiful young women died in posh resort hotels in the 1920s. In Miami, security broke into the victim's locked hotel room; the Pink Lady often locks her door, forcing security to break in. In Miami, the murderer fled into the bathroom; the Pink Lady bolts bathroom doors.

Are these coincidences? "I think it's a bit too much coincidence," Warren says. "If it said Grove Park Inn instead of the Flamingo

Hotel, this could be the explanation of the Pink Lady."

One possible interpretation is that Dorothy Frady checked into the Grove Park Inn after death. It wouldn't be a first. The Jekyll Island Club in Georgia is haunted by someone who died elsewhere.

But Bennett thinks its more likely the Pink Lady may be signaling *how* she died. "It could be that the Pink Lady's death was never recorded, and she's saying, 'This was the scenario. This is what happened.' "

A third possibility: The article is a complete coincidence.

"Probably the most challenging aspect of researching ghost stories is looking for the truth behind the story," Warren says.

Only one truth is clear here: The Pink Lady is one guest who's decided to face eternity with a room-service menu in hand.

If you want to stay in room 545, make reservations well in advance. The Pink Lady's popularity is on the rise. She's most active in cool weather and likes cheerful, even innocent people, so enter smiling.

It shouldn't be hard. The Grove Park Inn is one of North Carolina's finest historic inns. It houses the world's largest collection of Arts and Crafts furnishings and one of the state's best restaurants, Horizons. Elaine's, the Pink Lady's favorite nightclub, is open Thursday through Saturday.

Asheville

A popular mountain resort since the early 1800s, Asheville has more than its fair share of spirits—possibly because so many of its old buildings still stand, possibly because the area is so scenic that people just don't want to leave. Area attractions include the Blue Ridge and Great Smoky Mountains, the Blue Ridge Parkway, the town of Cherokee, and Biltmore Estate.

Many Asheville innkeepers say privately that they host ghosts. The following inns publicly admit to having them.

A supernatural game of billiards, heavy footsteps on the stairs when no one is there, and doors mysteriously opening and closing are just a few of the strange happenings at Biltmore Village Inn.
COURTESY OF MARGE TURCOT

Biltmore Village Inn

119 DODGE STREET
ASHEVILLE, NC 28803
800-963-4197 OR 828-274-8707
$$$$

Marge Turcot didn't believe in ghosts when she moved into this historic house in 1973. But after spending her first night in what turned out to be one of Asheville's most actively haunted bed-and-breakfasts, that began to change.

"The very first night we stayed here, we were awakened by the sound of heavy footsteps on the stairs. Actually, I thought my daughter was sneaking her boyfriend upstairs," Turcot laughs. But when she investigated, she found all the doors locked and her teenage daughter sleeping like an angel. "She was sound asleep. There was nobody where they weren't supposed to be."

Turcot looked for a logical explanation every time she heard the heavy footsteps, but to her chagrin, she never managed to find

Mr. and Mrs. Samuel Reed on their wedding day
COURTESY OF MARGE TURCOT

one. "It's never been scary, but it's totally unexplainable," she says. She and her family heard the footsteps most often when a new person was staying in the house. "I'm a nurse. I believe you take this test, and it comes back yes or no. Everything's black and white. To get into a realm of something totally unexplainable, that you couldn't put your finger on—it was very puzzling."

In fact, many puzzling things have happened here over the years. Turcot, a past president of the Preservation Society of Asheville and Buncombe County, was often awakened by the sound of a supernatural game of eightball being played in the billiards room. She and her guests would hear the rack break, the smack of the cue ball, the clatter of balls hitting the corner pockets. The

This photo of Mr. and Mrs. Reed was made in St. Augustine, Florida, in 1892. Some believe it is Mr. Reed who is playing billiards in the hereafter at the inn. Others believe it is his wife, who sat at home while he played eightball with George Vanderbilt at Biltmore Estate.
COURTESY OF MARGE TURCOT

balls would sometimes be left on the table in midgame. The only thing missing was players.

Some people believe that Samuel Reed, who built the house, was racking them up from the Other Side. Others believe it was his wife, who sat at home while Samuel played billiards with George Vanderbilt at Biltmore Estate. "People have theorized that Mrs. Reed comes back to play pool," Turcot muses. Children have been heard scampering up and down the stairs. Some people think these were the Reeds' children, five of whom died here.

Turcot is the first to admit she doesn't know who made the sounds, or why. "Guests often [come to] breakfast with stories of hearing weird sounds, without having any knowledge of our past and of the ghosts here," she says. "Lots of times, when somebody comes here for the first time, somebody will say, 'Hey, who was going up and down the stairs in the middle of the night?' We've had doors opening and closing and lights turning on and off. There are so many things. There have never been any sightings." And there have never been any logical explanations, though heaven knows she looked. "A lot of things *could* have been, but when we check them out, it never was," Turcot says.

What are your chances of meeting a spirit here? That remains to be seen. A company called 1892 Biltmore Village, LLC, recently bought the property. Following a total renovation, the Biltmore Village Inn reopened in January 2001 as "an upscale bed-and-breakfast inn," says managing partner Connie Munden.

The inn has five guest rooms in the main house and two in the cottage, a wraparound porch, fireplaces in the bedrooms and four of the bathrooms, limousine service, and landscaped grounds. Rates include a full gourmet breakfast.

You may want to request the Biltmore Suite, which includes the area once occupied by the billiards room, where those midnight games were played. The suite includes fireplaces in the bedroom and bathroom, a two-person whirlpool, and a two-person shower.

Be sure to let the new innkeepers know if you hear any spirits knocking about. "I'm looking forward to meeting the ghosts," Munden says.

The Grove Park Inn and Spa. Please see the feature on page 142.

Ghost researchers say WhiteGate Inn and Cottage registers extremely high electromagnetic readings, indicating high spirit activity.
COURTESY OF WHITEGATE INN AND COTTAGE

WhiteGate Inn and Cottage

173 EAST CHESTNUT STREET
ASHEVILLE, NC 28801
800-485-3045 OR 828-253-2553
www.whitegate.net
$$

Who haunts this inn? That's the question owner Frank Salvo is trying to answer with the help of ghost researcher Joshua Warren, who says the house has some of the highest electromagnetic readings he's ever encountered.

"I've heard doors opening and closing for a long time, our bed warmer rattling, things like that," Salvo says. "Sometimes the lights go on and off. We have gas fireplaces turning off and on by themselves." Small things move around the house, disappearing in one room and materializing in another.

Salvo believes there may be two spirits in the house, one friendly and one troubled. The first may be Merriam Bridgett, who owned the house and died in it. "[She's] a very warm ghost, a very calm ghost," Salvo says. "Merriam is very much the caretaker of the home. As long as there are guests in the haunted bedroom, she's calm. The other ghost is very disturbed. You can walk into the basement and feel waves of energy hit you. It's almost nauseating."

Research continues, but until the situation is resolved, guests might like to do what Salvo does: avoid the basement and enjoy the welcoming spirit in the guest rooms.

The inn has three guest rooms, one suite, and one guest cottage. Fresh herbs from WhiteGate's herb garden often enliven breakfast.

Bald Head Island

Theodosia's

P.O. Box 5130
Bald Head Island, NC 28461
800-656-1812 or 910-457-6563
www.theodosias.com
$$-$$$

Some people believe the spirit of Theodosia Burr Alston haunts this modern bed-and-breakfast on Bald Head Island, but owner Garrett Albertson isn't necessarily one of them.

Theodosia, the daughter of Aaron Burr and wife of South Carolina governor Joseph Alston, disappeared in 1812 while sailing from Charleston to New York. "Her ship never arrived," Albertson says. "It was either attacked by pirates or shipwrecked."

According to legend, whatever happened that fateful night made Theodosia lose her mind. "The stories seem to agree that she escaped to an island on the Outer Banks of North Carolina—probably [near] Nags Head—and was taken in by a family," Albertson says. "One night, she ran from the house carrying a portrait of herself. The portrait washed up on shore, but her body was never found. The legend is she walks the [coast] from Charleston to Nags Head."

Has she settled in the inn named for her? "Stories have cropped

Some believe Theodosia Burr Alston haunts Theodosia's.
COURTESY OF THEODOSIA'S

up," Albertson admits. Several guests have reported ghostly experiences in the inn. "One story was that during the middle of the night, a finger wrote in the condensation on a mirror the word *pray*," he says. As the guest complied, a water spout approached the inn, jumped it, and spun away. The guest believed a spirit had written on the mirror to protect the inn. "We don't know if there is credence to the story," Albertson says.

"Others have indicated they've seen a ghostly apparition and [felt] sort of a benevolent presence. One lady indicated that there was like a chill that went through the room, and then there was a sense of someone tucking her in, but she was alone in the room."

One guest videotaped what appears to be Theodosia but may be an illusion. "We have on the first floor landing my wife's grandmother's wedding dress," Albertson says. The guest videotaped the dress, which is on a dress form. When she showed the video the next morning, "it appeared to have a face on the dress form," according to Albertson. "It seemed that probably we could account for the fact that there was a mirror nearby and it was kind of an optical illusion, but it definitely looked in the video that it had a face on it. . . . So people do routinely refer to the dress form and dress as Theodosia."

If Theodosia does haunt this ten-room inn, she probably enjoys the contemporary conveniences as much as the paying guests do. Theodosia's opened in 1994. Room rates include a full breakfast, and complimentary golf carts and bicycles. Cars are not allowed on Bald Head Island. The inn also offers golf packages.

Balsam

A friendly ghost lingers on the second floor of Balsam Mountain Inn, which was built in 1908.
Courtesy of Balsam Mountain Inn

Balsam Mountain Inn

P.O. Box 40
Balsam, NC 28707
800-224-9498 or 828-456-9498
www.balsaminn.com
$-$$

A ghost lingers on the second floor of this country inn, says owner/innkeeper Merrily Teasley, who began restoring the 1908 structure in 1990.

"It's a very friendly ghost," Teasley says. "We don't know anything about it except that it shows up in room 205. One night, it turned the doorknob in the middle of the night. One night, the ghost raised the window. It's only been two or three weeks since

Construction on the inn began in 1905, shortly after the railroad came through.
COURTESY OF BALSAM MOUNTAIN INN

the window incident, and those people knew nothing about the ghost, and so that was really strange. But each person that's told us about it doesn't feel threatened. They just comment on it." The ghost's identity remains a mystery. "Nobody that I know of has ever died here," Teasley says.

This inn became popular thanks to the railroad at the foot of the hill. "They started building [the inn] in 1905, shortly after the railroad went through here," she says. "This depot is the highest depot east of the Rocky Mountains. They had six trains a day that came to bring people to the mountains, because it was the coolest place you could get."

The hundred-room inn was then known as the Balsam Mountain Springs Hotel, named for the seven springs on the property. Guests filled their water bottles from a fountain in the lobby. "People would come and spend the summer," Teasley says. "They'd bring their families."

By the time Teasley acquired the inn, it had fallen on hard times. "It was boarded up and condemned," she says. "It took almost a year just to get the first two floors completely up to code and livable. Fortunately, it was on the National Register of Historic Places. It was wonderful to restore it."

The inn now offers fifty guest rooms, a library, porches made for rocking chairs, an outstanding restaurant—and one ghost whose identity remains a mystery.

Beaufort

Beaufort, a quaint seafaring town founded in the early 1700s, is thick with ghosts. The bus tour of its large historic district includes information on many haunted houses, two of which are now bed-and-breakfasts.

Guests at Cousins bed-and-breakfast have reported hearing giggling and footsteps upstairs.
Courtesy of Elmo and Martha Barnes

Cousins

305 Turner Street
Beaufort, NC 28516
252-504-3478
www.cousinsbedandbreakfast.com
$-$$

Guests at this very friendly 1855 bed-and-breakfast report hearing giggling and footsteps upstairs. But so far, no one has actually spotted a ghost.

Cousins was originally built in 1855.
COURTESY OF ELMO AND MARTHA BARNES

Not so next door at Martha's Collection of Spices and Gifts, a gift shop connected with the inn, and the home of innkeepers Martha and Elmo Barnes. In this building, built in 1820, the ghost is practically part of the family. He's often seen standing in doorways and peering out an upstairs window.

One bedroom in particular seems to be his. The ghost has stretched out beside (and on) women sleeping in his room and has noisily rummaged through their jewelry. Once, three family members heard him descending the stairs and—thinking it was the innkeeper—rose to greet him. The stairwell was empty.

Cousins has four guest rooms and serves a full breakfast. Elmo's cookbooks are for sale in Martha's gift shop, which is where you're most likely to meet this property's ghost.

Captain Sabiston built the Elizabeth Inn in 1857.
COURTESY OF ELIZABETH INN

Elizabeth Inn

307 FRONT STREET
BEAUFORT NC 28516
252-728-3861
www.beaufort.net/Elizabeth1.htm
$

This bed-and-breakfast, now owned by Al Woodard, a captain of the Cedar Island ferry, was once owned by another captain. John Sabiston built the house in 1857. Some say it's Captain Sabiston who tries to come home to the house today.

Many men of nineteenth-century Beaufort made their living on the sea. Captain Sabiston would leave his home and his beloved wife, Mattie, for months at a time to trade up and down the East Coast and beyond.

Whenever a Beaufort ship came home, the villagers rushed to the waterfront to see if the returning sailors had news of their loved ones. One night, Miss Mattie heard a ruckus on the waterfront in front of her house. Looking out her window, she saw her husband's

Supposedly it's the spirit of Captain John Sabiston who is trying to come home to the Elizabeth Inn.
COURTESY OF ELIZABETH INN

ship anchored on the harbor. Then she saw Captain John walking up the landing, swinging a lantern to light his way. Mattie ran to the front door and flung it open—but Captain John wasn't there. Thinking he must have walked around the house, she ran to the back door. Again, no one was there. She finally went to bed, confused and longing to see her husband.

Two weeks later, another ship came home to Beaufort. Miss Mattie, like the rest of the villagers, rushed to the waterfront. The ship's captain pushed through the crowd to Miss Mattie and delivered his sad news: Captain John's ship had gone down with all hands onboard.

When did Captain John die? On precisely the night his spirit had tried to come home to his wife.

Since then, many people have seen Captain John's spirit coming up the walkway, lantern in hand, and heard his weary footsteps on the front porch.

Current owner Al Woodard, who grew up in the house, says he's never met Captain John's spirit. "But I've been scared my whole life," he deadpans.

The Elizabeth Inn is located next door to the North Carolina Maritime Museum. Bicycles are available. Children are welcome.

Glendale Springs

A spirit named Rosebud inhabits Glendale Springs Inn and Restaurant.
Courtesy of Glendale Springs Inn and Restaurant

Glendale Springs Inn and Restaurant

7414 NC 16
Glendale Springs, NC
800-287-1206 or 336-982-2103
www.glendalespringsinn.com
$-$$

A spirit named Rosebud inhabits this historic inn. Some think she's an adult. Others think she's a child. But one thing's for certain, says innkeeper Amanda Smith: Rosebud is full of energy. She opens and closes doors, walks along halls, moves things, and turns televisions on and off.

My husband and I met Rosebud several years ago. We checked

in during the off-season and happened to be the only guests staying in the inn. In the middle of the night, we heard the distinct sound of a child running up and down the stairs. We were puzzled, since no one was supposed to be in the inn. We were doubly puzzled when we found the stairway deserted.

The next morning, Smith told us that a little girl who died here in the late 1800s likes to play on the stairs. "I think her parents built the [place]," she says.

Gayle Winston, who owned the inn from 1980 to 1994, agrees that Rosebud keeps busy. One of her favorite areas of the inn? The dining room. Winston recalls that on one occasion, an earlier set of innkeepers invited their bankers over for dinner to discuss a loan. "The table was set in the Arbor Room," Winston says, referring to the dining room facing the grape arbor. "The bankers sat down, and at that moment, the silverware, the glasses—everything on the table—started to shake." The innkeepers tried to stifle the shaking, to no avail. "The bankers decided they wouldn't stay," Winston laughs. "Needless to say, they didn't get the loan."

Another night, Winston was catering an out-of-town event and faced the daunting task of baking five hundred meringues. "I could only do twenty-four at a time, so I would have to get up every couple of hours to make a batch," she says. The double doors to the Arbor Room fasten at the top and bottom. She closed them. When she walked by, they stood open. She closed them again. When she walked back by, they stood open. "Every single time I passed, the doors would be open," she says. Finally, she gave up. "I just laughed and sort of waved, like, 'How you doing?' "

Rosebud keeps busy in other parts of the house, too, often walking in the halls and on the stairway. One man working alone in the house "heard footsteps coming down the hall," Winston says. He went out to greet his visitor. "He said there was nobody there, but the footsteps continued until they were three feet in front of him."

Room 5 seems to be Rosebud's favorite. The door has been known to open in the middle of the night, latched or not. "Sometimes she's in the room above it, in room 1," Smith says. Rosebud sometimes turns the television there on and off. "I have felt her presence, but I haven't seen her," Smith adds. "I plant flowers, like the impatiens named Rosebud, so she'll feel at home. And I name things on the menu for her, things I think she will enjoy."

Rosebud probably appreciates the gesture. Consider what happened to Winston one night years ago. A friend had made tiny flower arrangements for an event they were catering. "That night, I heard an incredible crash," Winston says. "It woke me up. It sounded like a refrigerator had fallen." Naturally, she investigated. "I could find nothing at all, except in the middle of the hall was a yellow rosebud."

This country inn has nine guest rooms, an interesting history, and a good kitchen. Rates include a full breakfast, afternoon tea, and access to the generous porches. Holy Trinity Episcopal Church, home of one of the well-known frescoes by North Carolina artist Ben Long, is located within walking distance; St. Mary's Episcopal Church, the site of Long's three other Ashe County frescoes, is a few miles away.

Lake Lure

Lodge on Lake Lure

Box 519
Lake Lure, NC 28746
800-733-2785 or 828-625-2789
www.lodgeonlakelure.com
$-$$

For years, this lodge operated as a retreat for highway patrolmen and their families. Former innkeepers Jack and Robin Stanier opened it to the public in 1990, and guests began mentioning their ghost not long after.

The Staniers checked with previous owners, who confessed that the very active but comforting spirit is that of George Penn. It makes sense, since the lodge was built in honor of Penn, a highway patrolman who died in the line of duty in 1937.

Penn often appears in room 4, where he calmly walks around

It is believed that the active but comforting spirit at the lodge is that of George Penn, a patrolman who died in the line of duty in 1937.
COURTESY OF LODGE AT LAKE LURE

For years, the Lodge on Lake Lure operated as a retreat for highway patrolmen and their families.
COURTESY OF LODGE AT LAKE LURE

the room and then exits—often through locked doors. "No one's been scared by him," Robin says. "They felt very comfortable with him. Everybody just thought he was a person walking in the room by mistake.

"The former innkeeper said she saw him all the time, and he was naughty," she adds. "She'd put towels out [for guests], and they'd be on the floor. She'd just scream at him and say, 'Get out of here.' But I only saw manifestations twice.

"One time was Christmas Day, and the full family was here. I'd really set the table up beautifully," Robin says, adding that she'd placed a pair of large, blue glass goblets on a side table.

As she walked in at one end of the room and a friend walked in at the other, Robin's daughter was talking about the ghost. "My daughter said, 'If there *is* a ghost here, I wish he'd do something. I'd like to see it.' At just this moment, one of these goblets picked itself up and threw itself against the wall—like fourteen feet away."

All three women saw it.

Another time, Robin was showing the lodge to visitors. "Just as we walked in the room, a flower arrangement sort of flew across the room," she laughs.

"Everybody else has just seen him sort of wandering around," she says. "They didn't feel any fear."

Robin has shown a photo of Penn to several people who have come face to face with the spirit. "They say, 'That's him, all right.' "

Although Penn is most often spotted in room 4, room 2 also sees its share of activity. "Always, people come out of this one room and say there is no toilet paper, where we just put toilet paper. I say, 'You're in room 2, aren't you?' " she laughs.

New innkeepers Gisela Hopke and Mary Lee Phillips took over management of the lodge on October 31, 2000, and so far haven't met George. "If he's there we want him to come out and welcome us as the new managers," Phillips laughs.

If he's still in the lodge, George Penn has chosen a pleasant place to spend eternity. The Lodge on Lake Lure includes fifteen guest rooms, a veranda, a boathouse, a great room with a fireplace, and a beautiful view of the lake. Rates include a full breakfast and a sunset cruise, with wine and hors d'oeuvres following the cruise. A four-bedroom house is also available to guests.

Lake Lure is located about twenty-five miles southeast of Asheville.

A dozen or so guests have seen a woman's gentle spirit standing in room 4, looking out the window of New Berne House Inn.
Courtesy of Marcia Drum

New Berne House Inn

709 Broad Street
New Bern NC 28560
800-842-7688 or 252-636-2250
$

Marcia Drum, co-owner of New Berne House Inn, doesn't believe in ghosts—well, most of the time. "Sometimes I think I see things moving out of the corner of my eye, and I suddenly become a believer again," she laughs. "So I have announced out loud, 'Don't bother me and I won't bother you.' "

She needs to say it most often in rooms 4 and 6, which have seen the most unusual activity, according to a published report by former innkeeper Shan Wilkins. Wilkins reports that a dozen or so guests have seen a woman's gentle spirit standing in room 4, looking out the window. Room 6 has its own stories. Objects sometimes disappear and reappear months later in unexpected places—

on the roof, in a guest's suitcase. Also in room 6, a maid in an old-fashioned uniform has shown up in the middle of the night to drop off fresh towels. The guests in room 6 commented on the incident the next morning, only to be told the inn doesn't employ maids in old-fashioned uniforms. The innkeeper couldn't argue with the evidence, though: the ghostly maid had left two sets of fresh towels in the room.

There is less activity in others rooms: children's hand prints appear on mirrors when no children have been in the house; objects materialize in odd places; sheets get tossed about vacant rooms; a closed piano plays random notes and pieces of music. Guests have recently reported seeing the figure of a robed man in the hallway.

Among the seven guest rooms here is one that includes a brass bed rumored to have been rescued from a burning brothel in 1897. New Berne House Inn is within walking distance of Tryon Palace and the rest of the city's extensive historic district. Rates include a full breakfast.

While you're in New Bern, you may want to visit the Henderson House Restaurant at 216 Pollock Street, where a little boy's spirit keeps things hopping. "When women are here, that's when things happen," says owner Matthew Weaver. Jamie, the ghost, sends glasses floating through the air (though he never breaks them) and likes to fiddle with women's necklaces.

Southport

The Brunswick Inn

301 East Bay Street
Southport, NC 28461
910-457-5278
www.brunswickinn.com
$$

The ghost in the Brunswick Inn isn't the kind you keep under wraps. He won't let you. "Sometimes it sounds like we're having a convention in the house," laughs Judy Clary, who owns

The Brunswick Inn is haunted by Italian street musician Tony Casseletta, who moved to nearby Wilmington in the late 1800s.
COURTESY OF THE BRUNSWICK INN

and operates the inn with her husband, Jim.

This twenty-three-room inn is haunted by Italian street musician Tony Casseletta, who moved to nearby Wilmington in the late 1800s. A harpist, Tony performed on riverboats that plied their trade on the Cape Fear River.

"He'd come down with the river pilots on the boats," Judy says. "One beautiful, sunny day in August, he went out sailing." The boat sank at Bald Head Island, which lies just off Southport. "Tony was the only one to drown in the mishap."

The musician has occupied the Brunswick Inn ever since. "You hear him walk the rotunda—it's usually just four heavy footsteps," Judy says. "He's great for locking and unlocking doors." In fact, he's locked the bedrooms so often that Judy has become expert at slithering through transoms to let guests back into their rooms.

What's he doing in those locked rooms? "He gets into people's underwear," Judy says. On one occasion, a couple checked in, changed clothes, locked their door, and left. While they were gone, Tony went into the room, took the lady's underthings from her locked suitcase, and placed them in front of the fireplace. His interest isn't limited to women's garments, however. "He swings both ways," Judy laughs. In another case, after a couple checked in, showered, and left for dinner, Tony slipped into their locked room and took the gentleman's boxers from the bathroom floor. That night, when the couple turned down their bed for the first time since they'd arrived, they found the shorts neatly tucked between the blankets.

"He haunts the library and one bedroom particularly," Judy says. She used to play beach music in the library when no one was home to discourage unwanted visitors—until Tony turned music critic and dropped a fan from the ceiling. Judy took the hint. "We play classical instrumental now at all times," she says.

Tony also slipped down to the basement one night to play a piano that was still in its carton.

Judy has struck up a working relationship with this charming ghost. In fact, she hands the sanctity of the house over to him every time she leaves. "I say, 'Keep the house safe, and we'll see you when we get back.' "

This Federal-style inn overlooks the Cape Fear River and offers views of Bald Head Island and the Oak Island Lighthouse. Rates include a homemade gourmet breakfast.

Wilmington

Although ghost stories are attached to several bed-and-breakfasts in this old port town, innkeepers here worry that ghosts may be bad for business. Hence, Wilmington's ghosts still officially languish in the closet.

Thalian Hall—the city's beautifully restored performing-arts center—is well known for its ghostly activity. It is the best place in Wilmington to catch a show *and* see a ghost.

If you're in Wilmington in late October, call 910-251-3700 for information on the Bellamy Mansion's Halloween History-Mystery Tour.

VIRGINIA

Virginia's long, dramatic history has created an atmosphere conducive to ghosts and ghost stories. You'll find haunted inns on the Chesapeake Bay, in the Appalachian towns, and everywhere in between.

One of the state's most interesting but least-known haunted inns is in Newport News, where innkeeper Barbara Lucas believes a benevolent spirit helps keep the home running.

The Boxwood Inn

10 Elmhurst Street
Historic Lee Hall Historic Village
Newport News, VA 23603
757-888-8854
www.boxwood-inn.com
$-$$

Miss Nannie: At Home in the Boxwood Inn

The Boxwood Inn was once the center of civic and commercial activity in Newport News, says owner Barbara Lucas. Today, it's the center of ghostly activity.

Businessman Simon Curtis built this twenty-one-room house in 1896 and lived here with his wife, Nannie, and their four children. A general store occupied the back of the ten-thousand-square-foot home. "They also had the post office and the hall of records in there. You could do some of everything here," Lucas jokes. "I think it was the forerunner of the mall."

Eventually, the house passed out of the family's hands and fell on hard times. After its furnishings were auctioned off for $4 million, the house went on the market. A fast-food restaurant bid on it, planning to tear it down. "We bid to save the house, and that's what we're doing," Lucas says.

She realized that a spirit came with the house before the carpenters lifted a hammer. "When we first bought the house, I arranged to meet some workmen here. In the process of waiting for them, I carried in things from the car. I dropped a large box of tools and cleaning supplies, and I broke my fingernail. I said out loud to the house, 'Now I'm going to need a fingernail file.' I don't know why I said it.

"I am standing there looking out the window, and there is a brand-new emery board—crisp, clean, and never used—in a house that had two layers of coal dust everywhere. I picked up the file and used it. And I said, 'Thank you. Now I could use a hundred dollars.'

"Now, I'm not going to tell you I found a hundred dollars," Lucas

The generous, enthusiastic spirit of Nannie Curtis helped owner Barbara Lucas in unexpected ways during the restoration of The Boxwood Inn.
COURTESY OF THE BOXWOOD INN

The spirit of Nannie Curtis, who liked to decorate and cook, seems pleased with the restoration of the inn.
COURTESY OF
THE BOXWOOD INN

says quickly. But after the workers left, she noticed her shoe making a noise as she walked, as if she'd stepped on a nail. "I look in the bottom of my sneaker, and there is what looks like a brass tack." She pulled it from her shoe and took it to a window. "It was a gold tooth," she says.

On her way home, Lucas made her first-ever trip to a pawnshop. "I was very embarrassed. I have this tooth, and I creep to the counter, and I said, 'Do you buy gold?' He growled back, 'What do you have? You selling your wedding ring?' I said, 'No, I have a gold tooth.' " The man examined the tooth. "He said, 'You know what this is? This is a decorative tooth that people would have installed in their dentures in the 1920s. It is solid gold.' " The dealer hemmed and hawed. Then he said, "The best I can do for you, lady, is a hundred dollars. And so he gave me a hundred dollars." It was exactly what she'd asked for.

What tooth fairy is at work here?

Lucas believes the generous, enthusiastic spirit of Nannie Curtis helped her with the nail file, the money, and several other items as restoration continued. "Nannie Curtis was a power dynamo," Lucas says. "She was the woman behind the man. She would do anything to help support the family. She would work in the store. She'd send the cook over to the train station to invite men over for a home-cooked meal. These sailors would come in and eat and leave their nickel on the table. I think she was the energy that was left behind.

She liked the things I like. She liked to decorate, cook. She loved people, and she liked guests. She loved her family. We are alike."

Nannie maintains an interest in the restoration of her old home, she says. Lucas remembers working on one particular room. "Every night, I would close the [room's] door, and every morning, it would be open," she says. "[Nannie] was always peeking in there to see were we done yet."

But it was another spirit who came calling the night Lucas invited folks to a fund-raiser for the home. "The neighbors all told me I should have a fund-raiser here to get [the restoration] started," she says. "So I had a Civil War ball and reenactment and grand dinner. I sold a hundred tickets. There was no electricity, so we had to have candlelight and lantern light. . . . I brought in as many mirrors as I could get. I borrowed from a friend these marvelous old candelabras. . . . You can imagine how gorgeous it was.

"We started off with mint juleps on the front porch and in the front yard." She had invited a reenactment group, the Beauregards. "We had the Beauregards come here dressed in their evening finery, and had an encampment on the grounds." The encampment made sense, since the Battle of Williamsburg was fought here. In fact, Lucas has found cannonballs in the garden and bullets beneath the house.

At dinnertime, she seated the guests. As the waiters ladled peanut soup, a guest stopped her. "He said, 'You've got to go out front. There's an older gentleman, and he wants to know where to check in,' " Lucas says.

When she went to find him, the gentleman had disappeared. A few minutes later, another guest said, "The gentleman outside who has the great costume on—can he be seated at our table?" Lucas said that he could. She went out to get him, but again he had vanished.

She asked the waiters to watch for him. They soon reported they had found the old gentleman outside and invited him in. "He won't come in," the waiters told her. "He said he needs to register."

For the third time, she went outside to greet her guest. For the third time, he was gone. "We never saw the man again," Lucas says. "He was an older gentleman with a cane. Three people saw him

Some of her guests met a spirit the night Lucas invited folks to a Civil War ball, reenactment, and grand dinner.
COURTESY OF THE BOXWOOD INN

and spoke with him. All he said was, 'I need to register. I need to check in. I *need* to check in.' "

Although he didn't sit down for dinner, the old gentleman may have inadvertently posed for photographs. "Many of the pictures taken at the dinner that night had a stripe of light in them," Lucas says. She thought there was a problem with the camera or the processing until she saw another set of photographs taken by a different photographer with a different camera. They showed the same light.

Your best chance of meeting a ghost here? Unless a reenactment is in progress, early morning presents the best opportunity. Guests often report hearing a knock on their door before anyone is up. Lucas believes it may be Nannie rousing the house for work. (The general store, where Nannie sometimes helped out, opened at six in the morning.)

Nannie's spirit permeates all at the Boxwood Inn. "I sense a great happiness in the house," Lucas says. "It's like, 'There's people here at last!' "

Restoration is still under way at the inn. The house currently has four guest rooms with private baths. Some rooms have fireplaces; all have queen-sized beds and antique furniture. Lucas serves a full breakfast; the restaurant serves lunch and tea. "People love to sit and have English tea," Lucas says. "We have a large veranda."

Guests interested in exploring the area's many Civil War sites can get information from the local visitor center; call 888-493-7386 or 757-886-7777. Many guests also visit Williamsburg, which is only six miles away.

ABINGDON

The Martha Washington Inn was built as a private residence around 1830 and became a finishing school for young women in 1854.
COURTESY OF WASHINGTON HISTORICAL SOCIETY

Martha Washington Inn

150 WEST MAIN STREET
ABINGDON, VA 24210
540-628-3161
www.marthawashingtoninn.com
$$$

A young woman wearing a long dress and muddy boots, the whisper of violin music, a misty shape floating down a darkened hallway—legend has it that the Martha Washington Inn is the refuge of several spirits, including a Civil War nurse still mourning her lost love.

The inn was built as a private residence around 1830 and became a finishing school for young women in 1854. Eight years later, it became a Confederate hospital. Most of the students went home when the war started, says bell captain Pete Sheffey, who doubles as the inn's tour director. A few of the girls stayed behind. One of them, Beth, may still tarry here.

Abingdon "was a stronghold for the Confederacy," Sheffey explains. "When Yankee troops invaded the area, Confederate soldiers were stationed all the way to the [local] salt mines. Lots were shot, and lots died." During the skirmish, the Confederates realized they had a traitor in their midst: a twenty-year-old spy, Captain John Stover. "The Confederates shot him," Sheffey says. "His horse ran down Plum Alley," which cut "plum through" the settlement and passed near the inn.

Meanwhile, Beth had gone to the well in front of the inn to draw water. "She heard the shooting, and so she ducked under the trees, she did, and ran back toward the porch. [Stover's] horse drug him down Plum Alley several hundred feet. Beth heard someone moaning and crying. . . . She went in and told the doctors."

The medics waited for a break in the gunfire. "When darkness hit, everything went totally silent," Sheffey says. The team moved out. "They found him laying seven hundred feet [inside] the grove by the Martha Washington Inn." The rescuers carried Stover to what is now the Napoleon Suite and put him to bed.

Beth stayed with the wounded man for the next three days, playing her violin to soothe his spirit. "At twelve-thirty on Sunday night, Beth ran to the top of the stairs and cried for help," Sheffey says. "When [the doctors] entered the room, he had died."

Beth prayed for him, he says, and an apparition responded. "The room lit up between twelve-thirty and one o'clock," Sheffey says. "They said something was standing in the room. They said the lady was dressed in pure white, in a mist or cloud. They said [there] was a real cold breeze. . . . [It said], 'You did your best to comfort him. He's well taken care of. Be joyful.' And the room went dark.

According to inn lore, the ghost of a young woman from the Civil War era has been seen here. She wears a long, purple dress and old-fashioned, high-buckle shoes with red clay on them.
COURTESY OF THE MARTHA WASHINGTON INN

"He came back to life for a few seconds. He was alive but still shaking. [He said], 'My pain is gone.' He died with a smile on his face, he did. He died on April 14.

"She was stricken the following year," Sheffey says. "She also died in 403, right above his [room]. She died on April 14 between twelve and one o'clock. She's one of the ghosts here. We've had security guards and employees here that have seen her. I've seen her myself."

According to inn lore, Beth has been seen in a long purple dress and high-buckle shoes with red-clay mud on them. The mud struck the employee who saw her as odd, since it hadn't rained in days. Legend has it that Beth floats up the stairs and into rooms 302 (where Stover died) and 403 (where she died). Some people have heard her violin.

The Martha Washington Inn enjoys a dramatic history. To learn more about the inn's stories, ask for Sheffey when you visit. He'll give you a tour and fill you in on the details. "We like to keep it a legend," he says. "We're keeping it fun."

The Martha Washington Inn offers a dining room, a croquet lawn, tennis courts, a pool, and golf facilities. Packages with the historic Barter Theatre (which is also home to a very active ghost) are available.

Although one of the Linden House ghosts has been given the boot, a couple of his quieter friends still reside here.
COURTESY OF THE LINDEN HOUSE BED-AND-BREAKFAST PLANTATION

Linden House Bed-and-Breakfast Plantation

11770 TIDEWATER TRAIL
CHAMPLAIN, VA 22438
800-622-1202 OR 804-443-1170
www.bbhost.com/lindenhousebb
$-$$

Although one of the Linden House ghosts has been given the boot, a couple of his quieter friends still reside here, says innkeeper Ken Pounsberry. "We think it's two ghosts because of the voices—male and female. I've determined the sex [only] within the last five years."

No one knows the history of these spirits or where they fit into the Linden House's story. The plantation was established around 1735. When the Pounsberrys began restoring it in 1990, the house was in horrible repair.

"It had sat vacant for thirty-five years," Ken says. "We rode past this place maybe fifty times. It didn't have any charm to it. The roadway was just a road between two soybean fields. It was desolate. It just didn't have any charm until you came to the house and looked it over. You could see the potential. We called the real-estate agent the next day."

He and his wife, Sandra, began working on the house in June 1990. They knew at once that they weren't alone. "Both Sandra and I, when we first started, we heard footsteps and conversations—little conversations. You don't know where the sound is coming from. It bounces everywhere. You could never, ever, make out what the conversations were about. It was kind of mumbling things, nothing decipherable. That's what we noticed first."

The second thing they noticed? Complaints from the builders. "Some of our contractors would say they misplaced tools and would find them in a place they hadn't been. Mischievous things, I guess," Ken says.

Ken and Sandra's first priority was to fix up one room so they wouldn't have to sleep in a motel. "We took the Lee Room," Ken says. "It's on the third floor and faces the front of the house."

Their first night in the room, they weren't surprised when light came in through the keyhole—after all, they'd left the hall light on. But "it was like something was getting in front of the light," Ken says. "I noticed it, and Sandra noticed it. It was like something was interfering with the light coming through the door. You'd have a little ray of light, and then it would stop, like something was against it." They covered the keyhole. "When we clogged up the hole, we thought, 'We're going to get some rest now.' "

Not quite. "The rays came across the ceiling, over the top of the door. It was like a breeze coming in and pushing the door. It would just come across the ceiling like a sunburst. We just couldn't ever figure that one out. We just said, 'Well, we don't know what's going on.' "

One night soon afterward, Ken was there alone. "I was sleeping. I dismissed the rays, and I was trying to rest. The rays took another effect." A light floated into the room. "It had no distinct design, but it was a noncharacteristic-type color, kind of a pinkish, whitish, creamish color—really strange. It floated on the ceiling, and it went further and deeper into the bedroom. Finally, it just stayed there most of the night. I've got a lot of faith, so I just said, 'Nothing is going to bother me.' I said my prayers and tried to go to sleep."

A couple of days later, Ken told Sandra about the event. "She said, 'I gotta tell you something.' She had seen something similar to what I had seen. She saw the rays and this dancing [light]."

A friend, an Episcopal priest, suggested that they exorcise the spirit from the house. "We did that," Ken says. They haven't seen the light since. "We still hear these voices once in a while. We don't talk about them. It seems like when you talk about things, it kind of excites things."

The Linden House includes two suites and five guest rooms furnished with antiques. The ballroom seats a hundred. Outdoors, visitors may stroll in the English garden, visit the stables, or wet a line in the stocked pond. Rates include a full breakfast; dinner is offered by reservation. Children over twelve are welcome.

Hampton

Chamberlin Hotel

2 Fenwick Road
Hampton, VA 23651
800-582-8975 or 757-723-6511
$-$$

Dr. Denise Threlfall, assistant professor of occupational and technical studies at Old Dominion University, came face to face with the Chamberlin Hotel's ghost in 1991. But she remembers the encounter as if it were yesterday.

At the time, she was working with Virginia Commonwealth University faculty members on an Elderhostel program. "I was coordinator for the site, which was the Chamberlin Hotel," Threlfall says. "One of the professors was always talking about the lore of Ezmerelda."

Ezmerelda is a spirit long rumored to haunt the Chamberlin, a

Ezmerelda is a ghostly guest at the current hotel, which was built literally on the ashes of the original site in 1928. This photograph shows the Chamberlin in 1900 before the 1920 fire.
COURTESY OF THE HAMPTON HISTORY MUSEUM

grand hotel literally built on the ashes of the original Chamberlin Hotel in 1928. Fire consumed the first Chamberlin in 1920, gobbling up the wooden resort spa in twenty minutes. "Ezmerelda was supposed to have been looking out the window, waiting for her father to come back from sea when the first hotel burned," Threlfall says.

Although no casualties were reported in the blaze, Ezmerelda has been a frequent guest of the current Chamberlin Hotel since it opened. She's most active on the eighth floor.

Naturally, Threlfall and her friends were curious. "We would go up quite often to the eighth floor," she says. At that time, that floor stood empty—halls of dusty storage rooms with a spectacular view of Chesapeake Bay. For months, Threlfall and her friends tried to meet Ezmerelda, with no success. But one night, their luck changed.

"It was November of 1991. We had had a dinner and an Elderhostel graduation," she says. Threlfall and several others decided to visit the eighth floor. The elevator doors opened, and they stepped into the dark reception area. "It was very eerie, because there were no lights except for the red exit sign," she says. "Several people who went up with us were just pooh-poohing the whole thing. I kept saying, 'You guys need to get out of here, because we are never going to see anything if you guys are with us.' " She was right. They saw nothing.

The group went back downstairs. But a few minutes later, Threlfall and three others—one a clairvoyant—returned, minus the skeptics. "We hadn't been downstairs more than ten minutes," she recalls. "We went back up, and the minute we got off the elevator, the whole atmosphere had changed. It was very cold. I said something about it, because I thought I imagined it, and somebody said, "No, you're right."

The group strolled the dark hallways, stopping to peer into several rooms. Nothing. Finally, they stopped to rest. "None of us were moving," she says. "Then I could hear this kind of foot-dragging. It was really weird. I said, 'This is really strange. I just thought I heard feet moving.' Someone replied, 'So did I, but I didn't want to say anything.' Then somebody said, 'Oh my gosh.' "

Threlfall looked toward the window. "I could see her very slowly appearing," she says. "People still think I need to have my head examined, but it was as clear as could be. She was beautiful, with long, flowing honey-brown hair." The young woman was wearing a long garment. "It was almost like a nightgown of the twenties—cotton, because it would have flowed like that." As she watched, the shape became clearer. "Someone else said, 'Are you seeing what I am seeing?' "

"I was really scared," Threlfall says. "She was just looking out the window and ignoring us. Her head would turn a little bit—she knew we were talking about her. Somebody goes, 'Her hair is so beautiful. Can you believe it is so long?' They started talking about her outfit, and it was exactly what I was seeing. In an instant, she vanished, and somebody said, 'Oops, she's gone.' "

Threlfall then realized again how cold she was. "I got up, and I held my hands over my face. It had been very cold in there." As she lowered her hands, one of her friends reported that Ezmerelda had rematerialized, placed her hands over her face as Threlfall had, and disappeared.

Fire consumed the first Chamberlin Hotel in twenty minutes in 1920. This historical photograph shows what remained after the fire.
COURTESY OF THE HAMPTON HISTORY MUSEUM

"I walked down to the ballroom. Somebody said, 'Your cheeks are blood-red, like they are burning up.' " Threlfall, who had never had her face turn red like that before, thinks Ezmerelda may have been communicating the heat from the 1920 fire.

"All of this transpired in fifteen minutes," she says. "There couldn't have been any projections or screens, because there was no electricity [on the eighth floor]. . . . It was so amazing, because I wasn't saying anything, but everybody was confirming what I was seeing. We went back downstairs, and everybody that we were telling thought we were crazy," she laughs. "It has been eight-and-a-half years, but I can remember exactly to the T what I saw."

The Chamberlin, located on Chesapeake Bay, has 185 guest rooms, a restaurant, and a lounge. Amenities include tennis courts, indoor and outdoor pools, bike and jogging trails, and exercise facilities. Visitors have the best chance of meeting Ezmerelda on the eighth floor.

Ghost lovers will find other sites of interest in the Fort Monroe area. The many spirits spotted at historic Fort Monroe include the family of Confederate States of America president Jefferson Davis, who was imprisoned here after the Civil War.

Overhome was a young man's surprise gift for his fiancée in the mid-1800s.
COURTESY OF OVERHOME

Overhome

130 LOVELACE LANE
HARDY, VA 24101
540-721-5516
www.overhomebandb.com
$-$$

Built in the mid-1800s, this home was a young man's surprise gift for his fiancée. As it turned out, the surprise was his. She didn't like the house.

The young couple never lived here, but according to legend, the groom used it as a party house for several years, says innkeeper Becky Ellis. One room upstairs saw a lot of cards dealt and a lot of money change hands. "The story goes that someone was cheating, and he was shot, and it killed him," she says. "There is a bloodstain upstairs on the floor."

It's in that room that people have reported odd experiences, says Becky, whose husband's family has occupied the home since the 1880s. "Jimmy's uncle Tom was a bachelor who lived here all his life," Becky says. "Several times when [Uncle Tom] would wake up, the cover was raised off of his feet. He would try to pull it forward, and something would pull it the other way."

Family members have long reported unidentifiable sounds in the house, and visiting parapsychologists have sensed ghosts. "They said, 'Well, we can tell you there are lots of spirits here, but they're all fun loving,' " Becky says.

The Ellises have never come face to face with any ghosts, but Becky *has* had to scold the happy-go-lucky spirits for their activity in the bar, which the couple installed during renovations. "Two times, items in the bar have been disturbed," she reports, noting that no one was visiting at the time. "There was not a cat in the house or anything." Once, items were toppled from a high shelf but not broken. Another time, "a tray of beautiful, heavy glass decanters was knocked over—some in the floor, some in the chair," Becky says. "And the decanters were not broken. We really don't know how to account for that." She scolded the spirits, telling them they were welcome in the house—but not welcome to be destructive.

The spirits apparently took her words to heart. They've been neater since. Recently, however, they've begun turning the lights on and off.

Overhome has four guest rooms. It is located ten miles east of Roanoke on VA 116. "We're surrounded by mountains," Becky says. The inn serves a full country breakfast.

This is a photo of the current owner's Uncle Tom, who lived at Overhome his entire life. Tom claimed a spirit in an upstairs bedroom sometimes played tug-of-war with his covers.
COURTESY OF OVERHOME

The owners of By the Side of the Road Bed-and-Breakfast first became aware of unusual activity in the inn during renovations.
COURTESY OF BY THE SIDE OF THE ROAD BED-AND-BREAKFAST

By the Side of the Road Bed-and-Breakfast

491 GARBERS CHURCH ROAD
HARRISONBURG, VA 22801
540-801-0430
www.by-the-side-road-bb.com
$

Some people have heard ghosts, and a few people have seen them. Dennis Fitzgerald says he's touched one.

"It was during the construction phase of the house," says Dennis, who shares innkeeping duties with his wife, Janice. "We were renovating. We had just torn the house upside down. . . . It was ten or eleven o'clock at night. I was getting ready to go to bed, so I was going around the house and turning out the lights. I reached inside the interior stairway to the basement to hit the light switch. And I felt something grab my hand. It was just like another human hand, something actually grabbing me. It was probably a little colder than normal." He quickly decided to leave the basement lights burning that night. "I pulled my hand back, and I just went on upstairs. It was real quick—another human hand touching my hand."

The basement's renovation was completed soon after that, and the ghost hasn't reached out to Dennis since. "We've had other circumstances," he says. "There are always doors opening and closing when it's just the two of us around, when we don't have any guests. A couple of guests have heard things." So far, Dennis and Janice haven't found a way to predict the occurrences. "It just seems to come and go," Dennis says.

Whose ghost was on the basement stairs that night?

The Fitzgeralds opened their bed-and-breakfast in 1999. "The house was built in two sections—in the 1790s and 1840," Dennis says. He suspects the ghost may be connected to the home's Civil War heritage. "According to the history of the house, it was a field hospital," he says. "That's the only history I know of where somebody might have died inside the house."

He's more certain of the gender of the ghost who grabbed him.

The ghost of By the Side of the Road may be connected to the home's Civil War heritage. This is how the house looked in 1912.
COURTESY OF BY THE SIDE OF THE ROAD BED-AND-BREAKFAST

"I would think it was a man," Dennis says. "It wasn't a light touch. It just sort of covered my hand as I was going for the light switch. I guess that's another reason I would think it was a man—because it covered my hand."

The Fitzgeralds serve a full breakfast, as well as afternoon snacks on weekends. By the Side of the Road offers four guest rooms in the main house, plus a two-story cottage. "We do have one suite that is children-friendly," Dennis says.

Middletown

In addition to other odd happenings, a ghostly moan is heard almost every night at eleven-thirty at the Wayside Inn.
Courtesy of The Wayside Inn of 1797

Wayside Inn of 1797

7783 Main Street
Middletown, VA 22645
877-869-1797 or 540-869-1797
www.waysideofva.com
$-$$

This colonial-era inn has had plenty of time to rack up a ghost or two. "The Wayside Inn of 1797 is the oldest continuously operated inn in America," says owner Leo Macy Bernstein.

Employees of the twenty-four-room inn, located in the Shenandoah Valley, report lights turning themselves on and off at odd times, toilets flushing on their own, and other odd goings-on. But the most predictable occurrence is a ghostly moan heard every night at eleven-thirty. "Guests ask, 'What is that moan?' It's eerie," Bernstein says.

The moan drifts down from a sleeping loft in the oldest section of the inn, built in 1742. "Upstairs is about a three-foot space," says Bernstein. "There was a set of steps going up there. The straw is still there."

No one knows for sure who's moaning in the loft, but the innkeeper likes to think it's Lord Fairfax, an early guest. That's the story that has been handed down with the inn. But what would make Fairfax moan?

Money, of course.

"Lord Fairfax came here [from England] when he was in his twenties or thirties at the behest of his father, who had been given 550,000 acres of land by King George," Bernstein explains. Today, that land makes up parts of Virginia, West Virginia, and North Carolina.

But Fairfax's estate was shrinking at an alarming rate. "A dishonest land overseer was giving part of the land away, and selling it, and not compensating Lord Fairfax," Bernstein says. Fairfax hired a friend—a seventeen-year-old by the name of George Washington—to survey

The Wayside Inn of 1797 is the oldest continuously operated inn in America.
COURTESY OF THE WAYSIDE INN OF 1797

his empire. Bernstein tells guests they're hearing Fairfax moan over the lost land.

Fairfax and Washington did visit the old part of the inn. "We talk to George all the time," Bernstein says. A small bar is now located under the loft where the young surveyor may have slept. "People get to drink there a little bit, and they listen for Lord Fairfax at eleven-thirty." The moan is like clockwork. "I used to live in the inn. Every night at eleven-thirty on the dot, there was a moan."

It's a good story. But given the location—a loft over the kitchen—it also seems possible that the moaner could be someone less . . . well, lofty.

The newer section of the inn, added around 1900 and restored after a 1985 fire, has twenty-two guest rooms filled with antiques. Servers in the inn's seven dining rooms wear authentic colonial costumes and serve "fresh American cuisine."

Ghost lovers will also want to visit nearby Strasburg to check out Crystal Caverns, which is home to numerous active spirits connected with its Civil War history.

Newport News

The Boxwood Inn. Please see the feature on page 172.

Norfolk

Page House Inn

323 Fairfax Avenue
Norfolk, VA 23507
800-599-7659 or 757-625-5033
www.pagehouseinn.com
$$

The ghost of owner Stephanie DiBelardino's mother visits guests here from time to time—primarily to show off her antiques, DiBelardino says.

The Page House Inn opened a little over a year after Jean Martino, the mother of the inn's owner, passed away. COURTESY OF STEPHANIE DEBELARDINO

The Page House Inn opened a little over a year after Jean Martino, DiBelardino's mother, passed away. Martino had asked her daughter to take her china cabinet to the inn and keep it safe for her. "I set up the china closet just the way she had it set up," DiBelardino says.

She keeps the door to the closet locked—not that it makes any difference. Her mother, who enjoyed showing off her china in life, continues to show it off today. "Every once in a while, the door will swing open," DiBelardino says. "I mean, it's locked! She makes her presence known. It's usually when there are people she thinks will want to see her china, or who she really likes. That china closet is locked, and every once in a while you will see the closet door swing open, and I will close it, lock it, and it will swing open again. It doesn't happen at night. It happens during the day, when people are around."

Her mother's presence is very reassuring, she says. "She had

The ghost of owner Stephanie DeBelardino's mother visits guests at Page House Inn from time to time—primarily to show off her antiques.
COURTESY OF
STEPHANIE DEBELARDINO

Jean Martino asked her daughter to keep her china cabinet (seen here in the dining room) safe in her new inn.
COURTESY OF
STEPHANIE DEBELARDINO

said she was worried about her antiques when she died," DiBelardino says. "I think she is happy to know they're being very much enjoyed by the people who come here."

The Page House Inn, a fully restored, late-nineteenth-century in-town mansion, has held a AAA Four-Diamond rating since 1995. It's located in Ghent Historic District—an area known around here as "Georgetown without cars"—and is within easy walking distance of the Chrysler Museum of Art and the opera house.

The inn includes four guest rooms and three suites. A full breakfast is served; fresh-baked cookies, tea, and cappuccino are available to guests in the afternoon.

Sperryville

Conyers House Country Inn and Stable

3131 Slate Mills Road
Sperryville, VA 22740
540-987-8025
www.conyershouse.com
$$-$$$

The ghost in this country inn may be getting lonely.

"The house was clearly inhabited [by spirits] when we first moved here, and then you could see them be less and less active as we moved in," says innkeeper Sandra Cartwright-Brown, who owns this friendly inn with her husband, Norman. "They moved on—except for this one."

"This one" is the ghost of Sim Right. Guests report feeling his presence in the suite that bears his name. They say he's a jokester. "Sometimes things disappear, and then they are put back exactly where they should have been after you search for them very thoroughly," Sandra says. "We just laugh and say, 'Sim's busy again.' "

Guests have helped the owners identify the spirit. "We've had some people who are in the suite who have felt as though they

Sim Right, whose ghost is purported to be a jokester, lived at Conyers House from 1924 to 1964.
COURTESY OF ARLENE C. FRYE

have felt a presence," Sandra says. "Sim Right lived in the house, he and his extended family, from 1924 to 1964. And he was a dollar-a-year man. A dollar-a-year man is somebody who was only paid a dollar a year, but if he fattened three pigs, he kept one."

Sim Right seems to be enjoying his retirement. "Recently, we've found rocking chairs rocking by the fireplace," Sandra says. If it's not Right rocking, it's someone equally peaceful. "Whoever it is, he is benevolent," she says.

The main section of this four-story farmhouse was built in 1810. The front part was added by 1815. Conyers House serves a full breakfast. Horseback riding and fox hunts are available to guests for a fee. Pets are also welcome for a fee.

The spirit that lingers at Glen Coe Bed-and-Breakfast comes back to check on her roses.
COURTESY OF THE GLEN COE BED-AND-BREAKFAST

The Glen Coe Bed-and-Breakfast

222 NORTH STREET
PORTSMOUTH, VA 23704
757-397-8128
www.glencoeinn.com

Your best bet for meeting a ghost at the Glen Coe Bed-and-Breakfast? Try the rose garden, advises owner Anne McGlynn. "There is an old lady who haunts the gardens," she says. "She's in her eighties. I haven't seen her myself. Some of my neighbors have. And she, I guess, had a rose garden there at one time. She comes back to check on the roses."

The ghostly lady's concern is understandable. "With the renovation of the house, the garden was completely pretty well destroyed, and we are starting all over again," McGlynn says. "There hadn't been anyone in the house for a long time, and nothing had been done in a long time. We've already started to put in the rose garden. This is a very Victorian house. It just seems appropriate that there should be roses."

The spirit's love of roses reaches beyond the garden gate. "There also seems to be a waft of rose perfume that you get even in the wintertime," McGlynn says. "You tend to smell it mainly in the main entrance hall. That's where I've gotten most of the feedback from my neighbors who have come in. They always said that the house has a distinct perfume." The home's old wallpaper, which dated to around 1920, featured roses, and McGlynn has put roses on the walls again.

The Glen Coe Bed-and-Breakfast has three guest rooms. Rates include breakfast.

The museum across the street has a very active ghost. You may be able to see her in one of the upstairs windows. In fact, she recently accosted a group of men who came into her yard to cut a storm-damaged magnolia. "She shouted down at them to leave her tree alone," McGlynn chuckles. Later, when the men went inside to visit the museum, they asked about the old woman upstairs. Of course, there was none—but they recognized her from a portrait on the wall.

Staunton

Belle Grae Inn

515 West Frederick Street
Staunton, VA 24401
888-541-5151 or 703-368-9999
www.bellegrae.com
$-$$

Michael Organ doesn't doubt the identity of the spirit who haunts his inn. "Mrs. Bagsby is truly the mistress of the house," he says. "She's the woman who created the concept back in 1883, and I think her spirit remains today."

Mrs. Bagsby, who raised her family here in the late 1800s and early 1900s, particularly enjoyed one room whose windows overlooked the city. "It was referred to as 'Mrs. Bagsby's Haunt,'" Organ says.

Unfortunately, a recent renovation blocked the room's view, as well as its outdoor access. "There is no way for Mrs. Bagsby to get out of her haunt because they closed up all of the windows that overlook the city. When they closed that up, the only entrance was a spiral staircase downstairs, and *that* was removed," Organ explains.

Her last option for entering and exiting her favorite haunt? "A portal in bedroom number 7," Organ says. The portal has no doorknob or latch on the outside. "It's way up on a wall. You'd have to have a ladder. You can only access it from this side." But that doesn't stop Mrs. Bagsby, who frequently enters there and leaves the portal ajar.

The spirit of Mrs. Bagsby particularly enjoys the room whose windows overlook the city. The room is referred to as "Mrs. Bagsby's Haunt."
COURTESY OF BELLE GRAE INN

"When we opened in 1983, we were the first people to make this place come alive again," Organ says. "Everyone who's lived in this house, of which there have only been four [families], have been fun and big families and [have held] lots of reunions. It's just a jolly place. And when it is at its jolliest, it is not uncommon to find the door to Mrs. Bagsby's Haunt open."

Gatherings that recall the late 1800s, when Mrs. Bagsby was in her heyday, tug at her most. "It seems like whenever there is some sort of a fun gathering, particularly surrounding barber-shop music, that door that's going up into Mrs. Bagsby's Haunt is open. I think she just enjoys a good time," he says.

Mrs. Bagsby may also be a practical joker who enjoys unlocking doors. "The door to the basement uses a skeleton key," Organ says. "It's been locked for a year, and the key is not in the door. The housekeeper, for wintertime, had put paper around the top to keep the air from going through. Mysteriously, we got home, and the door was open. There is no way it can be opened, and it was. We just have no idea how that door got open. We couldn't even find a key to lock it again," he laughs.

She may also have taken a dislike to one frequent guest. "We have two hot-water heaters that service the inn, and all of the water runs continuously through all of the bathrooms," Organ explains. "There is a gentleman who is not as jolly as we would wish, and many times when he is trite or anxious or a son of a gun, he won't get hot water, and everybody else will."

This seventeen-room country inn is furnished with antiques, keepsakes, and period reproductions. "We have lots of canopy beds, four-posters," Organ says.

If you want to try to catch Mrs. Bagsby swinging in from her haunt, ask for room 7.

The inn has a restaurant and serves a full breakfast.

The ghost that haunts Thornrose House at Gypsy Hill has told guests her name is Caroline.
COURTESY OF THORNROSE HOUSE AT GYPSY HILL

Thornrose House at Gypsy Hill

531 THORNROSE AVENUE
STAUNTON, VA 24401
800-861-4338 OR 540-885-7026
www.thornrosehouse.com
$

No one knows the history of the spirit associated with this house, but the innkeepers do know her name. "She spoke to only one person, and that's the only time she gave her name," says Suzanne Huston, who owns the inn with her husband, Otis. "A young couple that was staying with us en route to Georgia, she spoke to him. . . . He said, 'I woke up in the middle of the night, and a woman was standing in the middle of the room.' He said, 'Who are you?' She said, 'Caroline.' And she disappeared.

"After that, two other times at four-month intervals, we had two other people in that room who had unusual things happen. We had not discussed it with anybody," Suzanne says. In the first instance, a man reported waking up to see his bedroom curtains part and the window open and close. "Another woman announced

It appears Caroline has calmed down since a not entirely artful closet in her old room has been replaced.
COURTESY OF THORNROSE HOUSE AT GYPSY HILL

it was haunted," Suzanne says. "She said, 'There's a nonmalevolent female spirit in the room.'

"The third time was the kicker," according to Suzanne. This time, she saw the activity with her own eyes. "We had had a couple of little, weird things that had happened to us that we couldn't account for." For instance, keys would disappear from other rooms and turn up in Caroline's. "We would laugh it off," Suzanne says. "One day, I went into that room and every electrical appliance was on—fan, heater, exhaust." And that's when she began to believe she had a spirit in the house.

The Hustons managed to correlate Caroline's arrival with an event: they had added a not entirely artful closet to her room. Could that have disturbed her? "We removed the closet," Suzanne says. "We took it back down and repaired the plasterwork and put all of this rubbish out." Caroline calmed down.

"I don't know if she's still here or not," Suzanne muses. "But if she's still here, she's calm. I do talk to her, particularly if I go up into that room."

Suzanne has researched the home but hasn't found anyone named Caroline associated with it. "A child died of rheumatic fever in that room," she says. She has learned that the child had a live-in nurse and wonders if Caroline may have been that nurse.

Thornrose House offers a full breakfast, afternoon refreshments, an acre of gardens, and verandas. Ask to stay in Caroline's Room.

WILLIAMSBURG

This beautifully restored village, Virginia's capital from 1699 to 1780, was the seat of Britain's colonial power in America and the birthplace of ideas that shaped the young United States. In its taverns, businesses, homes, and courts, George Washington, Thomas Jefferson, Patrick Henry, and other patriots plied their trades and argued their causes.

In 1926, John D. Rockefeller, Jr., spearheaded Williamsburg's preservation. Today, the Colonial Williamsburg Foundation oversees eighty-eight original buildings, plus hundreds of reconstructed homes, shops, government buildings, and other structures.

As you might expect, many spirits linger in Colonial Williamsburg, the world's largest living-history museum. Colonial Williamsburg offers overnight accommodations in twenty-seven different buildings. Two have been home to unusual happenings, says Steve Erickson, hotel manager of the colonial houses.

The Brick House Tavern

302 B FRANCIS STREET (CHECK-IN DESK)
WILLIAMSBURG, VA 23185
800-HISTORY
www.colonialwilliamsburg.org
$-$$$$

Most guests like the accommodations at the Brick House Tavern, but there's an exception to every rule. "This particular guest will never stay in the Brick House Tavern again," Steve Erickson sighs.

"The Brick House Tavern is a reconstructed building, but the

At least one guest at The Brick House Tavern has encountered an eighteenth-century soldier in her room.
COURTESY OF VIRGINIA TOURISM CORPORATION

foundation was original," he explains. "This guest said she was sleeping in a bedroom on the second floor. . . . The corridors are carpeted. She said she heard the front door open and shut. That's no big deal. There could be another guest in the house. She said she heard boots walking on a wooden floor." The woman, a frequent guest up to that date, described them as "soldier boots like they would have worn in the eighteenth century—big, heavy boots," Erickson says. "She heard him walk down the hall, up the steps, and then down the hall toward her room."

The guest, who remembered that the tavern's floors are carpeted, became alarmed by the impossible sounds. What happened next did little to soothe her.

"Her guest-room door was locked," Erickson explains. "This soldier enters the room, and she's seeing this apparition. It doesn't speak or anything. It comes to the foot of her bed and floats up over her, through the roof and away.

"She relocated that night," he says.

In fact, she has refused to stay here since.

The man's uniform was that of "one of the eighteenth-century regiments," Erickson says. "It was a militia uniform." The militiaman had the right house. "During the eighteenth century, this was a lodging tavern, and they did use the downstairs for little offices. The rooms above were reserved for gentlemen," Erickson says.

Today, the tavern's sixteen rooms are reserved for guests of all types. If you hope to meet the spirit, ask for an upstairs room.

The Colonial Williamsburg Foundation oversees eighty-eight original buildings, plus hundreds of reconstructed homes, shops, government buildings, and other structures. One of these buildings is the Governor's Palace, pictured here.
COURTESY OF VIRGINIA TOURISM CORPORATION

The Orell House

302 B FRANCIS STREET (CHECK-IN DESK)
WILLIAMSBURG, VA 23185
800-HISTORY OR 757-229-1000
www.colonialwilliamsburg.org
$-$$$$

Little is known of the early history of this eighteenth-century gambrel-roofed house. There's no record of anyone dying here. Still, at least one family had a very unusual experience on the premises.

"The [family] had the whole house," Steve Erickson says. "The parents were staying downstairs, and the children were upstairs." The next morning, the very perplexed head of the family came to Erickson. "He's a doctor, and not one to believe in supernatural kinds of things," Erickson says. Consequently, the physician had a hard time explaining his family's experience.

"They were all watching television in the downstairs living-room area, and they heard the water running in the bathroom," Erickson says. The father naturally assumed someone had left the faucet running. "The father got up and went into the bathroom and turned the water off." He then rejoined his family. "They heard the water come on again. This was weird because he knew the children were with them and all the doors [to the outside] were locked. It's not like someone could sneak in, turn the water on, and sneak out. He went back in the bathroom and turned the water off. This happened a third time, and he said, 'What in the world is going on?' "

The house has "a firm faucet," Erickson says—one that couldn't open by accident.

The family settled back in to watch television. "Then they heard a glass break in the bathroom," Erickson says. "He went *back* in the bathroom. . . . The medicine cabinet is one with a clip, and couldn't come open by itself." Nonetheless, it was open. A drinking glass had been removed from the cabinet and unwrapped. "The [glass's] plastic bag was out on the sink, and the glass was broken on the floor across the room, as if it had been thrown," he says.

The family took the scene in stride. "They all went to bed," Erickson reports. "They woke up the next morning. The children went into the bathroom upstairs. They went down and got their father and brought him up. Someone had taken the toilet-paper roll and strung toilet paper all over the bathroom. There was toilet paper everywhere."

The incident involving the doctor's family is the one and only report of this nature from the Orell House, Erickson says. "Guests don't tell us frequently that they've had experiences like that."

TENNESSEE

Tennessee doesn't claim as many haunted inns as some Southeastern states, but the mountain village of Rugby, founded as a utopian community in the 1880s, more than makes up for any dearth of spirits in the Volunteer State.

Newbury Inn

TN 52
Rugby, TN 37733
423-628-2441
www.historicrugby.org
$

Spirit-filled Rugby

Most towns are born of necessity: a need for protection, commerce, companionship. Not Rugby, Tennessee. Rugby was dreamborn. Its dreamer? English reformer Thomas Hughes.

In 1880, as Europe's poor flocked to America, Hughes founded Rugby as a colony for the English gentry's younger sons—educated young men facing a thin future in England, where their older brothers would inherit the family wealth. They felt right at home in Rugby, with its bowling greens, lawn-tennis grounds, ornamental gardens, bridle paths, homes, shops, and church. While America hammered railroad spikes and strung telegraph wire, Rugby's citizens poured themselves a spot of tea, chatted about the latest novels, and perused the *London Times*.

Several ladies claim to have awakened to find the apparition of Charles Oldfield standing at the foot of the bed.
COURTESY OF HISTORIC RUGBY, INC.

Enter Charles Oldfield, who now haunts room 2 of the Newbury Inn. Oldfield landed here as a spy, says Rugby's executive director, Barbara Stagg. "This was a gentleman farmer sent over to Rugby around 1882 to come into the community as just another settler and report back to some of the members of [Rugby's] British board," she explains. "He was living at Newbury, which was a boarding-house in the truest sense. To make a long story short, in the process of this reporting back . . . he, in essence, fell in love with Rugby. He decided he wanted to move his family here and become part of the community."

Oldfield bought a piece of land and wrote to his wife and son, urging them to pack their bags and sail for America. "His last couple of letters talk about having the arrangements made, and a lot, and so forth. [He says] he hopes his wife is getting ready to come to America," Stagg says. Oldfield wrote a little about himself, too. "His letters also report he is ailing."

Oldfield's son arrived first, only to be greeted by dire news. His father lay dying. "His son arrived the day that he died," Stagg says. "He was there to be at his bedside. In his obituary . . . it is mentioned that he was speaking of his wife as he passed on. They had a very sweet and dear relationship."

In fact, that tie seems to have outlived Oldfield, who still occupies his room in the Newbury Inn. "The story is that several women have reported . . . the ghost of Charles Oldfield," Stagg says. "Several ladies . . . have claimed to have been in bed, in room number 2, and awakened to find the apparition of a male figure standing at the foot of the bed."

Some of these women were visitors; one lived here before the inn was restored. One guest reported the figure bending over her. "They felt no fear. They said it was an overwhelmingly sad experience," Stagg says. "[He] didn't speak, but just materialized and awakened them by his presence. They felt it was a very, very sad and melancholy presence."

Guests have also reported activity in other areas of the inn. "I've had plenty of people say, 'I heard the ghost,' " Stagg says. A couple of instances particularly impressed her.

The first involved the room across the hall from Oldfield's. "It was bedroom number 1," Stagg says. A guest awakened around "three or four in the morning and thought he was hearing voices. About 5 A.M., he was awakened again, and this time, he *knew* he was hearing someone telling him that it was time to get up: 'Roland, it's time to get up now.' " The guest's name wasn't Roland, but he sprang out of bed. He and his wife "got up and looked all over the house, went out on porches, seeing if there was someone around. They were there for three nights, and it happened all three nights. Why him, I

The spirit of Charles Oldfield, who landed in Rugby as a spy, haunts the Newbury Inn which is shown here in an early photo.
COURTESY OF HISTORIC RUGBY, INC.

have no idea," Stagg says. "We've never had anybody report it again."

Another guest had an eerie experience by the parlor fire. "She didn't see [the spirit], but it walked up to her and laid a hand on her shoulder," Stagg says. "She felt it, and she smelled a very intense scent of old-fashioned perfume." The pressure on her shoulder was very distinct. "She just kind of froze. After a few minutes, she could feel the presence leave. Again, nothing scary. It was very benign." The woman felt the spirit was "trying to get her attention." It worked.

The Newbury Inn's spirits have plenty of ghostly company in the restored village of Rugby. If you visit during the last weekend in October, Stagg suggests trying the ghost tour. "It does a good job of knitting together . . . Rugby as a place that . . . seems to be fairly spirit-filled," she says. But you don't have to wait for October to visit. Spirits putter about this historic community every day. "[That's] partly because it's so unchanged," Stagg says. "There's no commercial development. There's very little development of any kind."

What else might you run into?

For starters, a ghost in Victorian dress paces the halls of the house known as Roslyn. Barbara Stagg's late brother, Brian, who spearheaded Rugby's preservation, often saw her. Using old photos, he identified her as Sophie Tyson, a former occupant of Roslyn.

Sophie paces, but at least she doesn't snore. In the house once owned by the mother of Thomas Hughes, Rugby's founder, a snoring ghost habitually kicks the covers off of one of the beds.

And in the Thomas Hughes Free Public Library, the spirit of a German librarian still rustles about at night, fussing over Rugby's outstanding collection of old books.

Then there's the ghostly carriage driver, riding hell-bent for . . . where? Several visitors have heard the thunder of horse hooves and watched open-mouthed as a black carriage raced along a drive and careened into a dense woods. Even accepting the carriage and its driver as spirits, the route baffled witnesses. Why would even a ghostly driver urge his galloping horses straight into a woods? Archaeologists finally answered that question. A recent survey identified the carriage's course as an old Rugby thoroughfare, once open but long ago reclaimed by the forest.

Why does this utopian community harbor so much energy? Perhaps it's just the nature of the place. "There have been a lot of people down through the years that have been passionately determined that Rugby will be taken care of," Stagg says. "All you have to do is read the prodigious material we have from these colonists. [They felt] the same way we feel today. [They had] a fairly impassioned belief that this colony is really meaningful. Even though it didn't accomplish the utopian goals of the founder, . . . it's still worth protecting and preserving and sharing with people."

Profits from the Newbury Inn help support this nineteenth-century village, which operates as a not-for-profit historic site. The inn has five guest rooms (three with private baths) and one suite. Ask for room 2 if you'd like to meet Charles Oldfield. And don't overlook the parlor.

Rates include a full breakfast at the Harrow Road Cafe and high tea "on special occasions." If you visit in October, when autumn's colors crest, be sure to ask about the ghost tours.

Athens

Woodlawn Bed-and-Breakfast

110 Keith Lane
Athens, TN 37303
800-745-8213 or 423-745-8211
www.woodlawn.com
$-$$

The identity of the ghost in this nineteenth-century house remains a mystery, but innkeeper Susan Willis thinks it may be connected to the home's Civil War history. "This county was very divided [during the war]," she says. "There were not a whole lot of working plantations. I think there were the same number of Union as Confederate troops here." Even the area's churches were split.

The identity of the ghost at Woodlawn may be connected to the home's Civil War history.
COURTESY OF WOODLAWN BED-AND-BREAKFAST

One served Confederates and the other Union sympathizers.

The Woodlawn was built in 1858 from bricks made on the site. "It was going to be a Greek Revival home, but then the war broke out," Willis says, noting that the columns didn't quite make it to the front of the house. "It was very Georgian-looking until the 1940s."

Although no battles raged here, Athens bustled during the Civil War. "There was a lot of troop movement through here" for the major actions at nearby Chattanooga and Knoxville, according to Willis. Both armies established hospitals in Athens. The Confederates turned a nearby college into their medical facility. The Union army selected Woodlawn. "I do have bloodstains in one of the rooms that used to be the operating room," Willis says.

No one knows how many soldiers died here, but at least one may still walk the halls. "I've had guests say, 'I heard somebody walk up your stairs at two in the morning,' " Willis says. "We have had other guests say that the door opened in the middle of the night, when they know the door was locked. One man said, 'I *know* I locked that door, and I woke up and the door was wide open.' " Another guest reported hearing a voice and seeing a ghostly figure.

Reports of these activities have been commonplace for years. "We've had the inn since 1993," Willis says. "Right after we opened the inn, we had some folks stay with us. . . . The lady said, 'You-all have ghosts.' She was awakened in the middle of the night by this voice, and the voice said, 'How long will you be here?' And then the voice spoke again, and it said, 'How long will you be here?' She looked at the window, to see someone standing there. As she watched, the shape faded away."

Willis takes the events in stride. "They are just things that happen.

"There are sounds I hear all of the time," she says, adding that the sound of opening doors is most common at midnight or a few minutes after. "They are door sounds—loud sounds," she says, though she can never locate their source. She doesn't let the sounds bother her. "I feel like if this house *is* haunted, it's haunted with a friendly ghost."

Your best bet of meeting a ghost? Try the Scarlet Room or, as a second choice, the Rose Room.

Accommodations at this historic inn include a full breakfast and afternoon refreshments.

BOLIVAR

Magnolia Manor Bed-and-Breakfast

418 NORTH MAIN STREET
BOLIVAR, TN 38008
901-658-6700
$

This gracious Georgian mansion was built of handmade, sun-dried bricks in 1849. And it's the 1849 Room that sees the most ghostly activity, says Greg Rivers, whose mother, Elaine Cox, owns and operates Magnolia Manor. "That room kind of gives me an eerie feeling," says Rivers, who grew up here.

It's the 1849 Room at Magnolia Manor that sees the most ghostly activity.
COURTESY OF MAGNOLIA MANOR BED-AND-BREAKFAST

Rivers believes a spirit haunts this house. "My mom has had two separate incidents, one-and-a-half months apart," he says. Both occurred just after midnight. The first time, Elaine Cox was in her room on the first floor. "She heard the distinct sound . . . of someone walking across the room over her," he says. Thinking someone had broken into the house and was prowling the 1849 Room, she got out her pistol. The footsteps soon fell silent. "One-and-a-half months later, same thing," Rivers says. Both times, the house was deserted, the exterior doors were locked, and the alarm system was activated.

Rivers and his wife have had odd experiences here, too. Before they came down to dinner one wintry night, they checked the doors to the upstairs hallway. Since they were trying to conserve heat, "we made sure we closed all the doors that led into the main hall," he says. The couple descended the first flight of stairs and paused on the landing. "We heard the distinct sound of a door opening and closing. I couldn't tell which door it was, but it was an impossibility. I know we had just closed and checked all of the doors." They took the rest of the stairs three at a time.

Guests have so far reported no strange experiences here, but they often ask if the house is haunted. "Mom has been asked several times," Rivers says. "I'm thinking that they feel some kind of presence."

One thing is certain: This house has a strong historic presence. Union generals Grant, Sherman, Logan, and McPherson used it as their headquarters during the Civil War. In fact, Sherman slashed the walnut staircase with his saber.

Magnolia Manor is known for its gourmet breakfasts. Rates include evening refreshments.

JONESBOROUGH

Hawley House is the oldest house in Tennessee's oldest town.
COURTESY OF HAWLEY HOUSE

Hawley House

114 EAST WOODROW AVENUE
JONESBOROUGH, TN 37659
800-753-8869 OR 423-753-8869
Tennessee-inns.com/jonesborough/hawley-house.html
$-$$

The Hawley House is a good place to party with a few spirits—if you're male and if you like giggly working girls. "I think maybe the house had been a brothel at one time," says innkeeper Marcie Hawley.

If so, she says, this 1793 inn—the oldest house in Tennessee's

The sounds of giggling girls, along with slamming doors, have often been heard in the rooms upstairs—but only by men.
COURTESY OF HAWLEY HOUSE

oldest town—occupied a prime location. "The railroad track is right here, and the Masonic lodge is right across the street," Marcie laughs.

Whether the house was actually a brothel or not is unknown, but it is clear that the spirits here interact only with men.

"My husband and the workmen heard things before we moved into the house," Marcie says. "They would hear laughter. . . . Every time they came upstairs to investigate, there was nothing."

Soon after the Hawleys moved in, the girls greeted Marcie's husband, Rick. "He heard doors slamming upstairs" one time when the couple was alone in the house, Marcie says. Rick jumped out of bed and ran upstairs. All was dead quiet. He came downstairs. Again, the doors slammed upstairs. "This time, he came upstairs with his gun," she says. "Nothing." He went back downstairs, only to hear the doors slam yet again. Up the pajama-clad innkeeper dashed, gun in hand. "He stood in the hallway. He said, 'I don't know who you are, but I understand that you are upset, but everything is going to be okay.' " The doors stopped slamming. For that night, anyway.

Since then, numerous guests have heard them. "[The spirits] go out in the central hall upstairs, and they're chatting and giggling and laughing," Marcie says. "Then they go into the bedroom and close the door. I have had people ask at breakfast, 'Who were the people in the front room that were making so much noise?' "

Ghosts have long loved Jonesborough, occupying its inns,

homes, and civic buildings. "As old as this town is, it just makes sense," Marcie says.

Then came the blizzard of 1994. "From that time on, most people have not felt the presence of their ghosts," says Marcie, who thinks the blizzard actually stilled the ghosts. "The temperature went down so low and stayed so low," she says. "It's like they froze."

Marcie isn't worried. A ghost has begun rustling over at the 1797 Chester Inn Museum. "I'm sure one morning, a man is going to come downstairs [at the Hawley House] and say, 'Who is that making all that noise up there?' " she laughs.

If you hope to welcome the working girls back to the Hawley House, ask for a room upstairs. Be forewarned, though: so far, no woman has heard them.

This rustic inn, listed on the National Register of Historic Places, has three guest rooms and a grand room with a massive stone fireplace. Rates include a full breakfast and afternoon tea.

McMinnville

Falcon Manor

2645 Faulkner Springs Road
McMinnville, TN 37110
931-668-4444
www.falconmanor.com
$-$$

"Our ghost is definitely his own man," Charlien McGlothin says. "He doesn't appear on command." But he does appear frequently, walking along halls, stopping watches, and posing for wedding photos.

The McGlothins believe the gentleman haunting this beautifully restored Victorian bed-and-breakfast may be former owner Clay Faulkner, a flamboyant businessman who built the house for his wife, Mary, in 1896. The Faulkners raised five children in their ten-thousand-square-foot mansion. In the mid-1900s, the house

Clay Faulkner, a flamboyant businessman, built Falcon Manor for his wife, Mary, in 1896.
COURTESY OF FALCON MANOR

became a hospital and nursing home. By the time George and Charlien McGlothin bought it in 1989 and began a four-year restoration, it lay in ruins.

Clay Faulkner may have moved back in when the place started looking like home again. When the McGlothins opened Falcon Manor, Charlien's mother occupied Faulkner's old room. She soon began hearing someone walk down the hall at night and stop outside her door. She didn't believe in ghosts but often laughed that it was Faulkner and that he was too much of a gentleman to enter a lady's quarters.

Today, that same room is a guest room, and Faulkner doesn't hesitate to step inside. Guests often find unusual energy in the room. "Every three or four months, something odd happens," Charlien says. Guests claim that their things are moved around the room and that the hands on their watches freeze inside the room, only to begin ticking again once they step outside the door.

Clay Faulkner may have recently attended a wedding at Falcon Manor, appearing as a white blur in several rolls of film.
COURTESY OF FALCON MANOR

In life, Faulkner showed a flair for advertising. He promoted his mill's "Gorilla Pants" as being "so strong even a gorilla couldn't destroy them." Apparently, he hasn't lost his love of publicity. Charlien says he recently attended a wedding at Falcon Manor and posed for the photos. "The white blur appears in photos from several rolls of film," Charlien laughs.

If Faulker has come home, he's probably proud of Falcon Manor, which claimed the National Trust for Historic Preservation's Great American Home Award in 1997. The inn has several antique-filled suites and guest rooms. Request Mr. Faulkner's Room.

It was the sound of footsteps walking steadily down the hall—an impossibility, given the hallways' renovation clutter—that convinced the owner of Prospect Hill that the sounds came from another dimension.
COURTESY OF PROSPECT HILL BED-AND-BREAKFAST INN

Prospect Hill Bed-and-Breakfast Inn

801 WEST MAIN STREET
MOUNTAIN CITY, TN 37683
800-339-5084 OR 423-727-0139
www.prospect-hill.com
$-$$

Judy and Robert Hotchkiss don't know exactly whose ghost walks the halls of this old Victorian bed-and-breakfast, but Judy has drawn some pretty firm conclusions about him.

"I have heard the footsteps, and I *swear* they were footsteps," she says. "They're hard-soled shoes. It sounds like a physically fit man who's about five-ten," she says. "There's no dragging footstep. It's a very steady-paced walking."

In fact, it was the footsteps' steady pace that told her their owner wasn't strolling through our dimension. She first heard them in the summer of 1998, a few months after she and her husband moved into their new home. "Those footsteps started outside my room, went all the way through this hall, and through the back hall." Renovations were under way, and boxes, vacuum cleaners, and tools cluttered the hallways. "There is no way a person could have walked at an even pace going down that hall," Judy says.

She's also heard the same, even footsteps on the interior stairs. "It was up and down the stairs," she says.

When she asked the former owners about the ghostly footsteps, they confessed that they'd repeatedly heard them. They'd also seen doors opening and closing by themselves.

Who walks these halls? No one knows. Perhaps it's Major Joseph Wagner, who had the house built around 1889. Or perhaps it's a restless member of the Rambo family, which occupied the house for seven decades.

Prospect Hill's six guest rooms include one two-bedroom suite. The inn serves a full breakfast.

Rugby

Newbury Inn. Please see the feature on page 207.

Sevierville

Little Greenbrier Lodge

3685 Lyon Springs Road
Sevierville, TN 37862
800-277-8100 or 865-429-2500
www.littlegreenbrierlodge.com
$-$$

A former innkeeper watches over the Little Greenbrier Lodge. "Margretta Craig used to own this lodge," says Charles LeBon, who owns and operates the bed-and-breakfast with his wife, Susan.

Margretta Craig, a former innkeeper, watches over the Little Greenbrier Lodge.
COURTESY OF LITTLE GREENBRIER LODGE

"Margretta Craig was a very staunch Christian lady. She died in the early nineties."

The LeBons accidentally photographed their ghost soon after they bought the lodge. "We had a photographer taking pictures for our brochure," Charles says. "They take black-and-white pictures to make sure the camera's set where they want it. In one of the pictures, there was a ghost in what was her room.

"It looks kind of like a little wave of light on the film," LeBon says. "It looks like it could be a person standing there, kind of white and milky-looking."

Today, the photo hangs in Margretta's room—where she may still spend quite a bit of time. "Good friends of ours have stayed here, and they said somebody grabbed their feet in the night," Charles laughs. "She's a good ghost. She opens and closes doors. You'll be out on the porch and come in, and she'll close the doors upstairs."

The LeBons and their guests have had other inexplicable experiences in the house, and they're glad to relate them to people.

LeBon's wife Susan emphasizes that this is a very pleasant spirit. "I asked God to bless every room of the house, so I know He wouldn't want anybody bad there," she says.

The Little Greenbrier Lodge opened in 1939 and was restored

in the 1990s. It offers nine guest rooms, each equipped with a private bath. "We have antique furniture, knotty pine walls, and hardwood floors," Susan LeBon says.

The LeBons serve a full Southern breakfast and invite guests to help themselves to snacks: homemade cookies, tea, and coffee. No drinking is allowed in the public areas; children over 12 are welcome.

The lodge sits near the border of Great Smoky Mountains National Park, about 150 yards from the Little Greenbrier Trailhead. The lodge shuttle takes guests to other trailheads; picnic lunches are available.

The LeBons say they don't really believe in ghosts. But if *you* do, ask for room 6. "Room 6 is Margretta's room," Susan says.

A photographer taking pictures of Margretta's old room for a brochure captured this wave of light on the film. Some people believe it's Margretta.
COURTESY OF LITTLE GREENBRIER LODGE

INDEX